MI TEEL

BAE FOR PAY

To Jessa

Happy Birthday!

Melissa
Steel

First published in 2020
1

ISBN 978-1-5272-7247-7

A CIP catalogue record for this book is available from the British Library.

www.bymelissasteel.com

Chapter 1

Never make conversation with a sales assistant. You'll get into all sorts of trouble.

When I accidentally walk too close to one and activate their 'on' switch, I will inevitably be asked if I need any help in prescribed corporate speak, before they try to sell me anything from broadband to a sofa with all the charisma of an automaton.

As such, I have perfected the 'leave me alone' glare. It is hard to describe, but it is about three parts murderous rage to one part total apathy about everything. This is not explained in the customer service manual, which usually causes the assistant to short circuit and stagger away and on to their next victim.

I decided to employ this one Friday night in Divine Drinks. The business was part of a chain that had opened up a slew of little hipster bottle shops in the last few years, taking what little money us millennials had left after buying all our avocados. One of its most successful stores was this one in Beath, Edinburgh's hipster neighbourhood, where everything was being mercilessly gentrified. The notorious bar for drug dealers and gangsters that once stood in the lot Divine Drinks now occupies was no exception.

The brand had enough money to have its own free 'Mini Bar' as they called it in its quirky but chaotic shops. Amidst the boxes of wine stacked on the shopfloor to keep up with customer demand, there was a small tasting bar. It was made of oak and painted a glossy red, draped in cheap fairy lights; it wouldn't have looked out of place in any hipster pub in the land. It even had a couple of matching red leather stools, 'reclaimed' from a local miner's club when it shut down, according to one member's newsletter I received. Stocked with the latest offerings, the Mini Bar was always open for wine-lovers to wander behind and serve themselves a glass or two before browsing.

When I heard, "That's a nice wine," that Friday evening in Divine Drinks, my eyes had already begun to narrow in annoyance by the second syllable. I mean, I fully intended to buy the wine, but now someone who worked there had dared to try and cajole me into purchasing it, I could already feel a sour taste in my mouth developing. I really just wanted to be alone.

My eyes flicked away from the bottle I was holding to note his nametag - 'Dean - Wino Wunderkind' it read. I cringed at the gimmicky title, paired with his attempt at designer stubble and B-movie grin. I didn't know who to feel more sorry for in this situation: him or me. I was going to have to endure his attempts at customer service, but this was probably the fifteenth time he had had this conversation today - enough to drive you to drink, divine or not.

"I said, that's a nice wine," he tried again, popping back into my line of vision.

"Yes." I said. My glare became a stare, fixed on the wine as one looks at a portrait in a gallery - an added squint or two to emphasise how engrossed I was in the label.

"Do you like dry white wines?" he asked breezily. I treated it like questioning under oath in a police station; if I said I did, was he going to try and sell me the most expensive one in the shop, if I said no, was I destined to have to sit through a tortured sales pitch for sherry?

"Maybe." It seemed like the safest answer.

"I tried that one the other night. It's pretty good with a curry from East to West," he said in between shifting boxes.

"Oh, what kind?" I cursed myself for slipping into conversation, but we were talking about curry on a Friday night, the holy evening of the takeaways. Plus, East to West was always getting rave reviews for its experimental fusions, and I had been summoning up the courage to try something daring off the menu for the last couple of months.

"I like it with their Madagascan goat and haggis curry, but it would go well with their Mexican mole foo yung too."

"Dear God, send a rescue plane to evacuate me from this hipster neighbourhood," I thought.

Suppressing a slight gag, I said, "I might just stick to my korma from the Marvellous Mahal, but you do you." Then I wondered why I was engaging in conversation at all when the Mahal's delivery driver was surely wondering where I was by this time.

"A creature of habit?"

"Well, I come in here every Friday night at approximately 6.38pm, spend 20 minutes pretending I am deeply interested in all the flavours of the free wine on offer at the Mini Bar, walk about trying to convince myself that I am not going to buy the same Sauvignon Blanc I buy every week, buy it anyway and go home have it with a korma from the Marvellous Mahal. But you already knew most of that."

I had first noticed Dean in the store two or three months beforehand. "A transfer from our New Town branch now that it's getting busier," the manager Nigel had explained as he marshalled Dean around the store with a pricing gun and the air of a pompous policeman in a '70s sitcom. Slowly but surely, he had been allowing the man more freedom, or 'day release' as I thought of it, to ring through purchases by himself and even converse with customers.

"Well, who doesn't love a wine with a curry on a Friday night? And we're all guilty of oversampling the wine. Just to double check, not that it's the only thing that has stopped me whacking Nigel over the head with one of the bottles or anything like that. AHAHAHAHA," he babbled, clearly enjoying his newfound freedom.

"Of course," I could feel a smile spreading across my face.

"But...I've been wanting to try this wine," he said with a tragedy only found in classic Russian dramaturgy. "Yes, I've wanted to try it for so long," now the tone ebbed into James Bond and Bond Girl Number 2 - the one who would survive the film and never be heard from again. My interest waned.

"Well, why don't you try it, then? You work here - if you can't sample the wines then there is no hope for the rest of us."

"Well," he said, putting a bottle behind his back and furtively glancing around as if he was a shoplifter. "I can, but I need a customer to ask for a sample too," he added with a market trader wink.

"You need an enabler! Why didn't you just say? I'd be happy to return the favour. After all, you guys enable me every week with free wine."

The bottle was already open and the wine just hitting the bottom of the glass. "I'm glad you said that." He passed a rather generous glass to me. Normally I would go straight in for a glug, but I was aware that I was in an establishment with trained wine personnel, so should at least make an attempt to appear interested in its aroma and taste. I followed his lead and swirled the glass and sniffed deeply with only a few nanoseconds' delay.

"It's not bad," he muttered as if he had been asked to comment on a cup of tea in a greasy spoon. Still, this seemed to warrant a top up of his glass. "What do you think?"

"I think - it's wine. I think my standards are a lot lower than yours."

"Wine is wine, that is true. Don't get me wrong, it's a good wine, it's just I am surrounded by it all day, every day, so even good wine becomes 'not bad'."

"Such a hard life you lead."

"Well, it's not bad," he smiled into his glass.

"You know what, I think I'll take a bottle for tonight. Curry sounds...not bad at all."

"Good, I'll ring it up - after we finish our glasses," he winked, topping up the cups.

A little while later, I tottered out into the street. The fresh air hit me and so did the realisation: I had been had. Sure, I liked the wine and the company, but I felt a little used too. A man had used me to get his hands on some wine. I didn't have a problem with that in itself, but the transaction was not the one I had expected; it was not the simple tap of the card against the contactless machine.

There was a little give and take, a small measure of intimacy for a splash of wine, a quip for a sip and another streak of colour on the canvas that made this a real person, not just your partner in playing 'shops' like you do when you are a kid.

It was like haggling in a market, I thought to myself as I passed a giant buy-one-get-one-free poster for pizzas in a supermarket window. Both players knew the game and what they wanted at the end of it, but there was a little whimsy to proceedings, a coy denial of what was going on.

All that scheming had left me hungry for a curry.

Chapter 2

Not that it was all so calculated. In fact, I would even like to think that we - almost - could have passed as friends at times. One time, Dean even asked what my Instagram handle is, which is the modern-day equivalent of asking for your hand in marriage in some parts.

It was another Friday night and I was quietly helping myself to a large Zinfandel when I spotted Dean performing a vault over some boxes and heading straight for the wine counter.

"You look pleased to see me," I observed.

"But you don't look so pleased to see me."

It was true – I spotted myself in the CCTV video loop above us; I looked like a goblin stuffed into workwear. Hunched and scowling, I hung onto my glass of wine as if I was guarding it from those damn billy goats that kept stomping across my bridge.

It had nothing to do with Dean, though. It had been one of those weeks in the office and now I was reliving it all mentally.

I had spent many interminable hours compiling reports on the Metrics of Digital Media Asymmetry. I was the one who ran the reports and I had no idea what that meant, so trying to explain it seemed a bit fruitless.

However, I had somehow managed to pull tens of thousands of words about it out of various orifices. It was not what I had always imagined for myself when I was writing from my almost literal ivory tower of my student days at the uber-privileged, many turreted St Fillan's University, a three hour drive to the north of Edinburgh. I had been a writer for the student newspaper, tapping away pithy opinion pieces for the chattering classes and features that always seemed to end up with me in a compromising position, crawling through a field to escape a herd of cows or almost being elected the new local councillor.

Somehow annual reports had never quite figured in my grander schemes. Yet there I was, trying to summon the inspiration to finish an introduction from the CEO with a jaunty sign off. I wasn't entirely sure why I wanted to make any effort, really; Sandra the CEO, a title she insisted on being addressed as at all times, took great joy in lacerating anything I composed. I knew it would be promptly scored out in red pen and replaced with something highly offensive about my writing ability or insinuating that I was a direct descendant of a government-controlled inbreeding experiment in the Outer Hebrides.

On top of this, Patience, the well-meaning if slightly dull HR Coordinator who sat next to me, had been inflicting a sort of verbal Chinese water torture on me for the last four years, drip-dripping the question 'What are your plans for the weekend?' Every week without fail, I joined the merry dance with an 'Oh, just chilling, you?' which usually covered everything from my wine purchase on Friday night to a subtle understatement of the full-blown existential crisis about what I was doing with my life that arrived like clockwork on Sunday night. She would then complete the exchange with a bland 'Oh, how lovely. I'll be doing the same." The whole process made me long to tell her I was planning a murder spree just to see if she was listening, or if she had an automatic pre-record setting to tell me how lovely it was and how she would be doing the same.

It had dawned on me that I must have been on this internal diatribe a while as my screen switched to black and I caught sight of my goblin-esque reflection. I searched in vain for the bright-eyed blonde who raised a quizzical eyebrow next to my opinion pieces that I used to write for the university newspaper back in the day, but the hair was darker, the eyes were duller and so was my mood.

I saw Sandra the CEO spearing her way down the hallway in her sexy Gestapo-style high-heeled leather boots, so I banged randomly on my keys to summon my screen again.

"How is the introduction coming along...Sharon? Suzie? Sarah?" She asked, even though we had worked together for four years and she knew my name was Sam - the nametag was also a bit of a giveaway.

"Almost done," I said, sitting erect next to the document, waiting for her verdict and bracing my stomach like a boxer anticipating a punch to the gut.

A silence dragged on, like we were at a cenotaph on Remembrance Day. I thought about all my fallen comrades, the other Digital Officers who had taken the challenge on before me, only to fall in the line of duty, doomed to run screaming from the building. My favourite story, although I am about 99.9% sure it was just a vicious rumour, involved one memorable, acrobatic instance, when someone apparently left a fresh turd in Sandra the CEO 's pigeonhole. I should have heeded their warnings and not signed up like a fresh-faced recruit in 1914, destined for a fine career as cannon fodder.

"Oh dear," she finally pronounced and began to walk away, I imagined to persecute some minorities or attend a World War II re-enactment, you know, one of those ones where they dress up as Nazis for 'authenticity', not because they are raging fascists or anything like that.

Yet I sighed, relieved. This was really quite mild for her, she must have been in a good mood. I walked over to the window, stretching out my back after a long day hunched over the desk. I arrived just in time to see Sandra the CEO leave with a much younger man. Not that she was terribly old, she was a well-preserved 45 at a push, I would estimate; she was like the chic renovated warehouse she had naturally gravitated to and set up her business in. I never felt very comfortable there, even when she wasn't on her crusade to completely erode my self-worth. The address was just off Edinburgh's Royal Mile in the Old Town, which has a castle at one end and a palace at the other, with quaint stone buildings straight out of an episode of Outlander in between. It was all a bit too posh and traditional for me. I would gladly hurry back to Beath at the end of my shift; it might have been full of affected millennials who worked in marketing, but then again, I was an affected millennial who worked in marketing and I liked that I fitted in a bit more there. Besides, I wouldn't want to ruin my nice glass house by throwing too many stones.

As I longed to return to Beath for the weekend, Sandra the CEO was taking part in her own Friday night ritual. Each week, a different toyboy would arrive in a flash car to spirit her away from the office. It was never the same one twice, I was pretty certain that she ripped their heads off and feasted on their young blood to maintain her youthful visage. What a woman she was - a cross between one of those female concentration camp guards all the soldiers fancied and a Praying Mantis. It would have been almost admirable if it wasn't so abhorrent, I thought as she confidently strode down the cobbled Old Town street in her ice pick heels.

Her victim of the week caught my eye as he held open the car door for her. I nodded at him sadly. He was very beautiful, like a Roman sculpture that had been forced into an ensemble from Superdry. It would be a shame for him to die - or whatever really did happen to the toyboys.

Not that I would tell Dean about any of that. He probably had to listen to the assorted woes of customers all day; he didn't need to listen to another episode of Middle-Class Disasters while consoling himself with increasingly stronger wines.

"Tough day?" he asked, waving a hand to get my attention.

I shrugged it off, slipping off the scum of the week like a grape shedding its skin. Dean didn't look convinced and tilted his head at me, the way puppies do when they don't understand what is going on.

Nigel, the manager, shambled out from the office. He was old enough to be our dad and looked as if he lived in a time capsule from the 1980s - only he had slightly outgrown that time capsule; his Levi jeans and Aerosmith t-shirt twisted around him like a sausage casing.

"Sam!" he wheezed, tired from his ascent from the stockroom, a whole flight of stairs below us. "You do the social media, right?"

"The social media?" Dean smirked.

"Yes, the social media. I accept no imitations," Nigel replied haughtily.

"I do," I replied shyly - it occurred to me Dean and I had never discussed what I did when not drinking wine. I dare say he even looked a little impressed – or maybe it was just the bouquet of the glass of Malbec he had somehow acquired that elicited that reaction. "Why do you ask?"

"We had Justine in from Gorgeous Gins earlier today..."

"Here we go..." said Dean, rolling his eyes.

"Justine is a lovely professional lady."

"She is also 30 years younger than you and on commission," muttered Dean. I suppressed a smile.

"Justine said I should 'check out' her...Instagram Story? Apparently you can't pick up a copy of one of them in a bookshop, and it all has to be done online." Nigel hesitated before offering up his phone.

"Would you like me to set up some social media profiles for you?"

"Yes, please," said Nigel, going as red as Dean's Malbec.

"Oh, you'll be an influencer in no time, Nigel. Selling protein shakes and looking buff!" said Dean, giving Nigel a playful push on his way passed.

"Give me a minute," I said *flipping open* Nigel's phone and trying not to look too horrified. It really should have been in a museum by this stage.

"Thank you, Sam," Nigel said coyly. "It means a lot to me - tell Dean you can have your bottle on the house tonight. Anyway, I'll leave you to it." He shuffled back to the office, though I swear there was a spring in his step.

Ten minutes later I approached the till, Nigel's phone in one hand and a bottle of wine in the other.

"Give this to Nigel. I think he'll be pleased - I made him 15 years younger and 20 pounds lighter with creative use of a few apps."

Dean picked up the phone. "You know, I'm tempted to send a few compromising messages to Justine, just to see if he finally has the heart attack he keeps threatening to have whenever a shipment is late."

"If Nigel has his way, I think it will be Justine who kills him off with a heart attack," I laughed.

Dean gave a half-hearted chuckle and held on to the bottle for several seconds.

"Dean, don't come between a woman and her wine," I cautioned.

"Sorry," he said, handing it over promptly. "You um..." he bashed a few keys on the keyboard and scratched his head with the pen that was perennially behind his ear.

"I um?"

"Are you on Instagram?" he asked, a tinge of Malbec appearing in his own cheeks.

"Me? No, not in 'real life'."

"Oh," he said, "That's cool. I just wondered. No big deal," he said, randomly pressing some more buttons.

"I really don't!" I laughed. "When you spend all day every day writing the perfect words for someone else, it doesn't leave much room for your own."

"That sounds a bit sad," said Dean, with what seemed almost like genuine concern.

"It does, doesn't it? Do you have a wine for that?" I asked.

"Go on! Go home before Nigel discovers Tinder," shuddered Dean.

Chapter 3

Week in, week out, my Friday nights would follow that same template and they came to be my social highlight of the week. Not that that is hard – the other contenders were the odd glass of wine with my friend June, trying to be as invisible as possible in the back row of gym classes and receiving three insults a day or less from Sandra the CEO .

Each Friday, I would sit in my office, watching the computer clock on its excruciatingly slow journey to 5pm. Then, as if I were still at school, an internal bell would ring in my head and I would spring from my seat and speed walk to the wine shop. If I was lucky, I would miss the start of Sandra the CEO 's mating/death ritual with her fresh-faced friend.

Due to such a hectic schedule, the festive season snuck up on me and I found myself scurrying about mid-December trying to sort out my life. First thing on the To Do List: cards.

Writing Christmas cards should be easy. Take a stack of cards that have the stamp of an inoffensive charity on the back and an equally inoffensive furry animal frolicking in the snow on the front, add the 'to' and 'from' to the inside and feel the relief of ticking another thing off the list.

At least, I imagine that's how it is for people who don't overthink things. First of all, there is choosing the card itself. Most of my friends have now started doing American-style family cards with them in their worst Christmas jumpers, their spouses and newborn children or dog surrogate children. Not wanting to feel left out, I made my cat, Lily, pose for a selfie, found a website that puts your photos on festive backgrounds and bang,

I too had an odious Christmas card to foist upon my friends and family. I could see the funny side and so could my cat, despite her glare in the photo, I was sure.

It seemed more fun than the standard jovial penguins and reindeer spattered across the card shop and I thought it showed I could laugh at myself, and also them, but I'd pretend that it was just the former.

Then the next stage: who to send the card to. There is the temptation to mail it to everyone you have ever met, just in case you offend someone. If you do that, you risk looking needy and bored though, like you're under house arrest and desperately want someone to come over and read your electricity meter, just to feel alive.

That's the position I found myself in as I debated sending a card to the wine shop. Best case scenario, they find it charming and kooky. Worst case scenario - I am a demented cat lady and they bar me for life. I would have to go to an off-license like it was 1990 and I was on a budget. Despite this foreboding threat, I eventually decided on nothing ventured, nothing gained and wrote the card. It then sat on my desk for several weeks while the internal argument continued.

As I went to place my Christmas wine order, I committed to putting it in my bag. I entered the shop and tried to look normal, all the while knowing that I was carrying something that would possibly put the cork in ever being tolerated in here again.

My nonchalance lasted all of thirty seconds. I made it through a casual 'hey' with Dean pretending that I was an extra in Grease - the ones that wore lots of leather and were apathetic about everything; you imagine that if they were told their entire family had been killed in a fiery bus crash, their only reaction would be a shrug of the shoulders and the lighting of a cigarette in tribute.

Thinking about Grease for a while was enough of a distraction to make me look semi-normal, but I knew it wouldn't last. I decided to throw myself into sampling the 'Special Christmas Selection' of wines on the bar, which had been decked out with some tired tinsel and a tiny Christmas tree. If nothing else, compulsively drinking wine gives you something to do with your hands and mouth in anxiety-inducing social situations that doesn't involve nervous tics or narcolepsy.

"The new Pinot Noir from Washington is supposed to be very good," Dean said absentmindedly as he unloaded another crate marked 'Christmas' in huge foreboding red letters.

"Supposed to be? You call yourself a wine expert! I demand a tasting this instant to resolve this mystery once and for all."

Dean gave an indulgent smile and I felt a pang of gladness that I paid a good portion of his salary, which probably saved me from an eye roll. "Ok," he sighed dramatically, tossing his industrial scissors to the side and stripping errant masking tape off his arms without a wince. Perhaps he really did want a glass of wine, or maybe there was a clause in his contract that he had to humour at least one sad woman a day. Then it hit me: I hadn't worried about giving them the Christmas card for almost three minutes. That was an achievement, even if I had accomplished it by worrying about something else.

"So, this wine is meant to be very festive and...romantic," the words were ruined by the fact the cork wouldn't budge, but after some resigned grunting, it slithered out. Dean turned the bottle so he could read the description on the back. "This is the first wine on the market from this vineyard. It's called Judy, named after the winemaker's first crush in Middle School in the early '90s. Apparently she moved to Wichita when they were 14 and he never saw her again.

"Meh."

"Meh? You've not even tasted it yet!"

"It always weirds me out when adults are still obsessed with their first loves. It leaves a bad taste in my mouth," I said, sceptically watching Dean pour out the light red wine for me. "Like, should we really be applauding a grown man who is so obsessed with an idealised 14 year old that he is naming a wine after her 30 years later? He should be on some sort of register."

"That's a good point, but I think most romantics look past that...issue."

"They're the same people who write fan-fiction about Lolita and Big Bird, if you ask me."

"Ok..." Dean poured himself an extra-large sample.

"I bet he wouldn't be interested in Judy, now that she is about 45. God forbid, she probably has wrinkles and the odd grey hair now that she isn't bouncing around a playground in pubescent glory."

"Ok, well, try and put the, er, 'pubescent glory' and pervy middle-aged men to one side and enjoy the wine," Dean said, sliding a glass across to me.

A man in a business suit on the other side of the shop glared in our direction.

"I have nothing if not an open mind. A wide-open mind, like a cavern. Brimming with judgment, but still, I'll try." I took a sip of the Pinot but the taste was tainted by the story.

And then I went back to worrying about the Christmas card. I had completely forgotten about it. I busied myself by swirling my glass, and while it took a lot of energy not to nervously fling it over my shoulder, the monologue of 'they're-going-to-think-you're-weird-they're-going-to-think-you're-weird' galloped around my head like horses on a demented carousel.

"What are you thinking?"

"Erm? About the wine? A little vinegary, reminds me of something you'd get in a church to absolve you of your sins. Like those sinful thoughts the winemaker has about poor Judy."

"That's a very...vivid description."

"Thank you, I'm surprised the words 'vinegary' and 'sins' aren't on the label."

"It's truly a mystery, isn't it? Well, the tasting notes say 'sour cherry and hints of liquorice.'"

"Oh please, 'sour cherry' is wine person slang for 'vinegar but I have to drink it.'"

Dean gave a little laugh - an almost genuine one - not like the usual gracious twitter he used on customers.

I would have thought more about that but then I started to worry about the card again. "I suppose I should get on with the Christmas shop then and let you unload those boxes."

"You're too kind, really."

Browsing all the other wines took my mind off what I was now convinced was my inevitable social suicide by Christmas card. However, once I was satisfied with my order list, I knew it was time to face the music and/or rejection and disgust.

But not quite yet.

Back to the Mini Bar I rode. The Judy red was still open but I still felt a bit icky looking at it, so I plumped for a nondescript bottle of plonk next to it. It wasn't quite what I would have had as part of my last meal, but it would have to do. Soon the cumulative effect of the wine began to take hold and I felt I could surf over to the counter on the wine-dark sea I was now floating on to pay for my haul.

I decided that, even if the Christmas card meant I was never allowed in here again, it would be worth it because it would commemorate the time and appreciation I had for the staff who had tolerated me. If this has to be the way I socially topped myself, then so be it.

"Oh, and here's a Christmas card for you," I said nonchalantly as I left, feeling very proud of myself. Then petrified. Then mortified. Then made Edvard Munch 'Scream' faces to myself once I reached the main street and knew they couldn't see me anymore.

Chapter 4

My parents stayed at mine over Christmas. I wasn't sure why - they were the ones who had retired to Malta. I never understood why we couldn't celebrate on a warm Mediterranean island rather than on a bitterly cold Beath street by a frozen dock that was in the news because they pulled at least two drunks a week out during the festive season. I didn't have much time to think about my Christmas card episode at the wine shop, I had a whole week of deflecting questions about what I was doing with my life to keep me busy in between the usual cocktail of gorging ourselves, playing Scrabble and watching various Christmas specials on TV.

This year's interrogation went something like this: How was my job going? Was there any chance of promotion? Was I going to my university reunion this year? Did I still speak to Harriet and Allan? They were a lovely couple. Did I have a boyfriend? Were many of my friends still single like me? Had I thought about investing in a holiday home? I could move there when I retired, you know.

There were a couple of times I thought going for a wee swim in the dock with the ill-fated revellers might have been a sweet escape, but Lily and I would roll our eyes together and I would ask who wanted more wine. The answer was always everyone and it provided a great diversion from discussing my life. With this tried and tested tactic no one died, and I waved them off at the airport with a sigh of relief a few days later.

The next week I approached the wine shop with a skulking anxiety normally reserved for when you face your work colleagues after a particularly hedonistic night out. It had to be done though, my friend June was having a New Year's party and I couldn't turn up empty handed.

"Sam!" chorused Nigel and Dean.

"Hello," I mouthed timidly, sidling towards the wine counter. Was that a smirk on Dean's face? An eyebrow raise from Nigel? Oh lord.

Back to old faithful, I busied myself with this week's samples. The Judy was languishing on the counter still and it gave me a cringing flashback to last week. Did I really bring up Lolita and Big Bird?!

I looked blankly at the rest of the tasting selection, not really taking much of it in, until something I saw something out of the corner of my eye. It looked a lot like my cat. And me.

"Oh my god! It's me! And Lily!"

"Of course it is!" said Nigel, appearing with a flute. "For your champagne. It's almost New Year, after all."

"I can't believe you put the card up!" I giggled as the bubbles zoomed up the glass.

"Why wouldn't we?" appeared Dean. "It's personalised – much better than that bloody corporate one we got from the gin company!"

"Oh yes," muttered Nigel, followed by a deep sip of his own champagne. "Dear Insert Shop Name, Christmas Greeting to be approved. Managing Director." Obviously there was trouble in paradise with Justine. He took another sip, but I was surprised anything could pass through his pursed lips. "The indignity."

"That's disgustingly mundane. Unlike this champagne. Very good selection, Nigel!" I said.

"Thank you. A little appreciation is all I ask for," he said with an indignant sniff off his glass, before retiring to the stockroom, most likely to mope over what might have been (in a million years, after an apocalypse, when hell had frozen over and the last male cockroach had died) with Justine.

"I fear he may be in there some time," said Dean.

"It's like his study. Every repressed middle-class man needs one, surely?"

"Yes, he's off to study the labels of cardboard boxes from around the world," what followed was at first a hearty laugh, like a studio audience, which turned into more of a shocked squeak. "I think I've seen my future."

Chapter 5

I had been worried enough about giving a card to the wine shop that I completely forgot to panic about the reception it would get from my friends and family. That was until I saw the name 'Harriet' flash up on my phone. Harriet and I had been best friends forever while we were at university, although that had fizzled out once we graduated. We had gone from flatmates who shared bras and bitching sessions to casual acquaintances who shared the odd-GIF or five-minute phone call for the latest gossip one of us had gleaned about classmates we ourselves hadn't spoken to in years.

Now my mobile was vibrating with the same delirious glee Harriet felt when she had something on someone. I answered, reluctantly.

"Hello there!"

"Samanthaaaaaa! I got your card last week, been meaning to phone you. So quirky. I love it."

"Thank you." I wasn't sure why I was thanking her though - 'quirky' was Harriet's euphemism for 'insane and/or a threat to the fabric of society'. She would probably describe Charles Manson as a 'musician with some quirky ideas' and Hitler as a 'quirky vegetarian'.

"I hope you liked ours. It's a bit more...traditional than yours but you were always a quirky character, weren't you?"

I didn't know exactly where I fell on Harriet's quirkiness scale - appearing on a Christmas card was the honoured position usually only reserved for subdued children on Ritalin or teenagers who had not disgraced the family yet, not your cat.

I obliged her with a non-committal laugh - because if she ever comes to any form of power then I'd like to survive the purge and not be dispatched with the rest of my 'quirky' brethren. "And how are you and Allan?"

"Allan is just great. So am I, of course."

"Of, course!" How could I have even dared to think otherwise?

There was some muttering and muffled phone noises, featuring 'it will be fine!' 'of course she won't mind' and 'don't question me'. With go-to phrases like that, you can see why I have my fears about her coming to power.

"Listen, we were just talking about going back to up to Saint Fillan's for the reunion. Do you want to come too? It will just be like old times. Allan agrees."

I had a very strong feeling Allan did, in fact, not agree, but knew resistance was futile.

"Let me think about it. It sounds...quirky," I smirked.

Now it was time for Harriet's non-committal laugh. "Well, let me know soon, I think it would do you good to go back. It has been a while now since all that ugly business-"

"What ugly business?"

"That's the spirit!"

I rolled my eyes almost loud enough for Harriet to see. The last thing I needed was a dose of her melodrama, that was the only ugly business I could see.

"I need to RSVP and it just wouldn't be the same without you. I'd just refuse to go. Even though we have already bought rather expensive train tickets. And I got a new evening dress specifically for the party. Oh, and we've paid our non-refundable deposit. Buuuut it's completely fine if you are busy...doing...whatever you're up to these days, I never really understand, is it something to do with Facebook?"

"Something like that, Harriet," I mumbled absentmindedly, already trying to formulate something decent to trump her emotional blackmail. Maybe there was time for me to sign up for a last-minute mission to a Cambodian orphanage?

The next week, the same time as always, I found myself in the wine shop, swirling a glass and mulling over the prospect of a weekend with Harriet and Allan, unable to come up with a decent excuse to avoid it. I had tried. I had asked Patience at work if any of her large brood of children had a cold they could give me, googled the best ways to fake your own death and even deliberately ordered a takeaway from a curry house with an alarmingly low food hygiene rating in the hope that it would give me some hideous tapeworm or other long-term misfortune. Alas, none of my plans had sufficiently incapacitated me.

I felt a little bad that I dreaded the idea of the whole thing so much. A few years ago, a weekend away with Allan and Harriet would have been the ideal break. Or perhaps not the ideal break, because it is what we did every weekend. There was always some wild adventure to be had at uni. It would usually involve ten pints, an escaped farm animal, a blow-up sex doll and, the great night out staple, a traffic cone.

Things had changed a lot since we graduated. Harriet, once the queen of chugging Guinness, would only politely sip kombucha at the most. Facebook photo albums used to be filled with us practicing our most awful ugly facial expressions, in some sort of misguided protest against girls who took selfies seriously. Now, the only expression Harriet practiced was one of disapproval when you did anything other than fetishise kitchen adverts or shop anywhere but Waitrose.

Allan I had never been quite as close to, but I remember that he occasionally had his own opinion about things and even looked at Harriet with a lovestruck gaze without being prompted. Now, he was more enigmatic than Mona Lisa, just without the smile and he now got a dig in the ribs to signal displays of affection.

"Is the wine no good?" asked Dean.

"What?"

"You just look like you've tasted something terrible."

"Oh no, the wine's fine. I'm just thinking about some friends."

"Are they friends if the thought of them makes you look like you've swallowed toilet water?"

"I had no idea I looked so radiant, thank you."

"Oh, all the gurning in the world couldn't hide your radiance!"

I laughed but rolled my eyes a little - sales must be a little slow this month. Probably an opportunity to turn my sour expression into cold hard cash.

"Radiant or not, I do have a problem. I've been invited to a university reunion by my friends."

"So?"

"They're a couple and the human equivalent of a weak cup of tea. I just don't think I can face going alone and having to spend three days with them with minimal alcohol."

"Just don't go, then?" Dean sympathetically topped up my glass.

"They are pulling a major guilt trip on me. Actually, that's unfair, one of them is as much as of a hostage as me in this situation, I fear."

Just then my phone buzzed on the counter. It was Harriet looking for her pound of flesh, right on cue.

"It's her! Oh god, I haven't even thought of an excuse yet!" I sipped nervously as the phone vibrated.

"Let me." I thought Dean was going to pour me some wine, but instead he picked up the phone and jabbed on speaker phone.

"Hello?"

"Oh er...hello! Is Samantha there?"

Dean mouthed a mocking 'Samantha' and said, "Oh she's otherwise engaged at the moment. I've just poured her a glass of wine, you see."

I veered between silent laughter, anxiety and mortification.

"Oh." I could hear kombucha being sipped through strained lips. "Sorry...who am I speaking to?"

"Dean."

"Dean." I could hear Harriet's brain whirring –where did Dean fall in the Big Judgemental Book of Baby Names she kept in her head?

"I'm sorry...I didn't know Samantha had a Dean," Harriet giggled coyly. She had obviously decided that 'Dean' was the right side of working class.

"Well, she does." I did another silent scream. Dean smirked a little, in a way that almost made me wish that I did indeed have a Dean, but this was soon replaced with a desire to exterminate him for the mess this charade would probably create.

I reached for the phone, but he reached quicker. He walked off with it, putting a pallet of wine between me and the phone. I took a deep swig of the glass and watched on nervously.

"Oh, how lovely! She never mentioned it, the sly fox. You sound like a lovely man."

Harriet only used the term lovely to describe things that brought her to an almost sexual frenzy: Getting into bed by 9pm, being right and any produce from the aforementioned Waitrose or a farmers' market.

"Thank you."

"Well, tell Sam to give me a phone back - actually, maybe you know the answer - what are your plans for the weekend of the 25th May?"

"Erm..."

"Oh good, you don't have anything planned! In that case, you can both come to St Fillan's! If I know Sam, she will have talked of nothing else but the reunion for weeks. It will be so lovely to meet you. Okay-thanks-bye."

Dean looked as if he was one of those people doing a 'sad face' in the newspaper because they had been conned or short-changed. I think I looked like a particularly demented Medusa. I was so angry that I could almost feel my hair launching at him like a swarm of angry snakes.

"What have you done?" I eventually sputtered. "How am I supposed to magic up a bloody boyfriend for this stupid trip?!"

"Look, I'm sorry, she's a slippery one." He was now backing away from me around a palette of wine.

"Ah – putting an obstacle between us! You think you're so clever but that's another big mistake. You've just given me some missiles to throw at you!"

"Not the '98 Chateau Bogart!"

I smacked the base of the bottle against my hand like a baseball bat.

"Fine, I'll sort it, just don't break that over my head! It's worth more than all my internal organs on the black market."

"That's not saying much, even your brain has obviously been pickled by the booze, judging by your little display just now." Still, I begrudgingly passed him the bottle.

"I will be taking this home to recover, though," I picked a bottle of the Judy wine. The thwarted romance vibes were appropriate - this fake romance was thwarting my chances at avoiding the reunion. "Actually, no, I can't, it creeps me out too much," I said, exchanging it for a nice safe Sauvignon Blanc.

Chapter 6

Some time later that evening, it was just me and the last loyal glass of wine left in the bottle. I released it from its screwtop prison and as the familiar splash hit the glass, things didn't seem quite as bad. I could survive the shame. I could order a crate of wine from the shop and just be in a permanent state of 'four glasses in' for the entire weekend. Dean might feel so mortified about the whole experience that he gives me a rather hefty discount too.

There was a knock at the door. I didn't move from the sofa. My takeaway had been delivered and eaten so no good could come of answering it. Then the knock came again. I muted the television and slunk off the sofa with my glass of wine. I tip-toed down the corridor and peeked through the spy hole. I could see the wine shop logo.

I sprung back from the door as what sounded like the base of a wine bottle rat-tat-tatted where my ear had been. And yes, I am that much of an oenophiliac that I could recognize that sound.

"Samanthaaaaa!" came the call from the other side, Stanley Kowalski-style.

"I know you're in there - I heard you wince when I hit the door with the wine bottle," came Dean's voice.

"What do you want? You've done enough damage for this evening," I said, inching back towards the door.

"I've come to make amends. I brought a bottle as an apology."

"Wine doesn't solve everything!"

"Sacrilege!"

"Ok, that was rash of me, don't tell Dionysus," I said, opening the door enough to peer round. I wanted to see what wine he had brought.

"Oh, the I'm Sorry Rosé."

The I'm Sorry Rosé was the latest brainwave from the wine chain's marketing department. Aimed at feckless men everywhere, it had doves of peace and roses on the front, the word 'Sorry' curling around them like a greeting card you would send to someone recently bereaved.

"I thought, 'if ever there was a time for this," Dean said.

"Indeed. You can come in, I suppose. I've never actually tasted fermented regret before, so it'll be a new experience."

Dean skulked round the door like a dog that has chewed something he shouldn't have. I started to feel a little uneasy - two parts of my life were colliding and I hadn't even had a chance to hoover. I took an assured swig from my glass and turned to face Dean defiantly in my living room. I was ready for war, even if I was framed by my pants hanging off one of those indoor washing line things on one side and the Christmas tree I still hadn't got round to putting away on the other. Boudica never had these problems, I thought.

We stood in silence, both looking at the muted television. Me, boring holes in it with my eyes, Dean, desperately seeking refuge from my wrath in an online bingo advert.

Finally, he summoned up the courage to speak. "I've er...I've got a plan. I feel really bad about what happened earlier."

I cackled as only one can after a bottle of white wine before falling abruptly back into the abyss of awkward silence.

"Look, this would be a lot less awkward if I was as drunk as you."

"I'm not drunk - I've had just the right amount. See, I haven't murdered you yet."

"Oh you are funny, even when you're threatening homicide," Dean said as he walked through to my kitchen as if he was in his own home. I imagined that this is what it was like for those women in 1950s TV shows when the husband comes home, but there was not enough wine in the world to tempt me to play the perfect housewife.

I could hear a drawer opening. "What are you doing?"

"I'm getting a bottle opener."

"But you don't know where it is!"

I ran through to the other room, an anxious hostess with my uninvited guest to find him piercing the top of the bottle with the corkscrew.

"You don't need to be Philip Marlowe to know everyone keeps their corkscrew in the cutlery drawer."

Next Dean opened the cupboard and pulled out a couple of wine glasses. They were a little dusty because I always use the same one, rinse and repeat as they say. The embarrassment was now strong enough to compete with the wine in my bloodstream and I loitered at the door as he gave them a quick run under the tap. Soon the sickly pink I'm Sorry Rosé was being decanted into the freshly cleaned glasses. It was the same colour as Cupid's vomit, but I tried not to think about it and just hoped it tasted better than it looked.

Dean handed me a glass and tried to maintain some manly dignity as he brought the luminous pink concoction to his lips. I likewise approached it with caution, but I wanted to at least appear like I was giving it a chance, so I gave it a cursory swirl and sniff. It smelt like an alcopop from your teenage years that had been left to 'mature' behind a radiator and lurched around the glass like an old gropey relative. I sipped it the same way I used to take unpalatable medicines as a child. The little liquid that made it into my mouth reminded me of mouthwash.

"Yeugh - you didn't tell me the 'I'm Sorry' part meant that they were sorry they had given it to you!"

Dean slammed a mouthful back as if it was a tequila shot. "It's truly disgusting, isn't it? At least it has an obscenely high alcohol content."

I held my nose and downed my glass. Dean looked a little scared. "What? I'm a middle-class millennial – of course I can down disgusting Rosé!"

"Good point – I should be a natural at it, then," shrugged Dean before gulping back the concoction.

"Ah, you too?"

"What do you mean? Do I not look young enough to be a millennial?"

"Mmm..." I considered his face. He looked like he didn't belong in this era. I always thought he would have suited black and white more; he was all monotone - inky hair and paper-white skin and a profile that was meant to be seen in shadow but was lost in full technicolour. At this point in my musings, I realized the Rosé was working and swerved away from the reverie.

"I just...never gave it any serious thought, I suppose," I shrugged with a sip.

"Well, I still like to think I'm a millennial, thank you very much," he poured himself another glass and mine too with a sort of automatic intimacy that sobered me up a little - but not for long.

"Sh...sh...I'm sure you are!" I almost ran my hand reassuringly down his film noir profile but managed to resist.

"How old would you say I am?" Oh god - the ultimate new acquaintances drinking question. I'd staggered into this drunken No Man's Land many times before and knew that the bombs would go off with the slightest nudge towards the wrong half-decade.

"I'm not even going there. No good can come of this."

"I'm 32. Do you know what Clark Gable had done by the time he was 32?"

Half of Hollywood, I thought, but decided to keep it to myself.

"He had got his big break. He was starring in films with Jean Harlow, he had been on Broadway, reviewers called him 'young, vigorous and brutally masculine'; not 'of indeterminate age and possibly easily offended'." Dean looked glumly into the shallow depths of his glass.

"Erm, well, I happen to know that Gable starred in It Happened One Night, by far one of the best films ever made, and won an Oscar within a couple of years of turning 32, so he hadn't even peaked yet. You haven't either."

Why had I said all that? Oh yes, the despicable Rosé of doom. I had unveiled myself as some sort of saddo with an intimate knowledge of Clark Gable and given a compliment without even considering the consequences.

"How do you know so much about Clark Gable?"

"You know while you were drinking in a park as a teenager? I was watching pre-code Hollywood cinema in some sort of prescient preparation for being an armchair expert at Pointless." Might as well be honest at this point, the wine whispered in my ear.

"Fair enough. You didn't miss much in the park."

"But how come you know so much about Mr Gable?" I leaned forward like I imagined a journalist interrogating a celeb on primetime TV, a female Parkinson. Then I slipped as I tried to lean on my knee and probably looked more like I had Parkinson's than anything else.

"Doesn't every man know a little something of Gable?" he said grandly, waving his arms like a drunken dandy.

"No."

"I know other stuff about Gable too."

"Oh?" I wasn't sure if this was genuine interest or slightly disturbed surprise - the demonic Rosé sort of smooshed feelings together like colours on post-cataract Monet.

"Yes – and Gable inspired my plan to help you," he nodded sagely, if blearily. I noticed he had produced another bottle of the god-awful Rosé from somewhere. He winked and tapped his nose, then began to stroke it. "Jesus, it's big, isn't it?"

"But Clark dearest had big ears and he made a success of things, didn't he?" I slapped the table as if it was a buzzer on a TV quiz.

Dean bashfully turned away and managed to spill the Rosé down his front. I was a little surprised that it wasn't corrosive and burned straight through. He looked down at himself like a bemused child with Ribena down their front. I began to wipe it - "Get that stuff off you - you'll probably go up in flames!"

"My plan! My plan! That's what we were talking about, right?"

"Yes! Yes! But I just remembered something else I know about Gable! I read it in one of those tabloid magazine supplements when I was like, 10."

"Why were you reading that when you were 10?!" said Dean, laughing, presumably at the image of Baby Sam flicking through the trashy story with wide eyes.

"I read everything - it was at my Gran's house and was more appealing than the bonkbusters and old-lady-investigates-a-murder books she had. Anyway," I said, staggering back to my train of thought, "Did you know that Clark Gable was allegedly gay for pay when he was trying to break into the business?"

"Urgh, you've stolen my idea," he said, flopping back in his seat.

"You were going to become a rent boy for rich men to stop me having to go to a reunion weekend with my friends?"

"No!" Dean said, clasping offended hands to his chest.

I huffed. I was actually a little disappointed.

"Well, you were half right. I, I will volunteer as your lover for the weekend."

"Erm, what? I think the Rosé is giving me auditory hallucinations." I held it away from me as if that would solve everything.

"Well, not your actual lover, but I'll go with you."

"No!" I retreated backwards into my seat, like a burrowing animal. I might have been completely plastered, but I still knew this was embarrassing.

"It's the perfect plan. We know enough about each other and we can sock it to your stuffy friends." This was accompanied by a lazy attempt at an 'up your jacksie' hand gesture, in which one arm represented an unfortunate bottom and a fist the weapon of justice.

"I don't think that's a good idea."

"Why not?" He said seriously, covered in pink wine and his head bobbing like a buoy.

"I'm not sure why," It was one of those questions - like the age one - it was better just to be polite about. Though the more I thought about it, I couldn't really think of a valid reason why, if he managed not to saturate himself with radioactive Rosé over the course of the weekend.

"Just consider it. I promise that I'm a good actor."

"Is Clark Gable a bit of hero, then?"

He smiled coyly as if he was talking to Clark Gable himself. "A bit, yes..."

"Did you want to be," I embraced the spirit of the wine flowing through me and affected the proud pose of a Shakespearean player, "an act-oooor?"

"A bit, yes," he said, followed by a coquettish sip of the pink satan juice, "I could have, in the words of Marlon Brando in that film I am too pissed to remember, 'been somebody."

"Oh em gee! Me too! I coulda been somebody too!" I raised my hand as if I was a swot answering a question in class.

"You wanted to act?"

"Not so much. I wanted to write something that isn't correctly punctuated corporate speak," I fell back into my glass.

"Ah! An authoress!" It was interesting to note that Dean appeared to regress to a different century after a few drinks.

"I always wanted to be Dorothy Parker."

"Isn't that a clothes shop?"

"No! That's Dorothy Perkins," I sniffed. "Dorothy Parker was a writer. She did witty articles and sketches about her life in New York. She is responsible for loads of famous quotes. You'll like this one: I'd rather have a bottle in front of me than a frontal lobotomy."

"So why don't you write, then?" Clearly Dean was also auditioning for the role of drunken Parkinson.

"I'm not very good," I said, feeling the spectre of Sandra the CEO looming over me.

"I'm sure that isn't true," said Dean confidently, though I think we had entered that drunk phase where everyone is an amazing shining unicorn who is surely going to rule the world with Beyoncé one day.

"Oh, it is," I said, taking a comforting gulp of the rancid liquid. "The last time anyone liked what I wrote, it was...let me think...I think it was Spring 2013," I said, taking another glug. "Actually, I remember it well. It was a satirical article for my uni newspaper. A travel article about going to Versailles and thinking, 'They had it coming.' Really pissed off a few of the descendants of the French Royal Family, all of whom were in one of my tutorial groups, of course. Apart from that though, everyone loved it."

"Jesus, where did you go to uni again?"

"St Fillan's," my eyes growing misty with memories, or maybe myopic with the drink. Memories of gate-crashing famous polo players' parties and champagne brunches on my friend Paxton's sailboat floated through my mind on the sea of wine.

"And you were surrounded by a bunch of toffs of all the time? How did you bear it?"

"It wasn't that bad. Some of them were actually ok, you'll like them," I admitted.

"Oh, I will, will I?" asked Dean. "Sounds like you are agreeing to my plan."

It was true, in the back of my mind, I had begun to swish the idea around like a wine - a slightly better wine than this nuclear nonsense. One that didn't make you want to spit it out and sign up for a tongue replacement immediately. He was a bit of an actor, he might be able to pull it off. A few days away with Dean in St Fillan's would probably be better than my normal weekend agenda , which consisted of laundry, changing Lily's cat litter, buying a lottery ticket and intermittent sobbing when said lottery ticket didn't win, followed by wine and FaceTiming June to ask her what I was doing with my life. I wrestled with the prospect a few more moments before swallowing it hook, line and sinker.

"Fine, let's do it," I said, throwing back the last of my glass.

"Cheers to that," said Dean. "I've just had another fantastic idea," he gasped as if receiving divine revelations from above.

"Let's become an actor and a writer - just for the weekend."

"Have they started selling these experiences online or something?"

"No - when we go away with your friends."

"Pretend?" I asked, starting to get intrigued.

"Yes! Now you're getting it! They have no idea who I am, and we can use a little artistic license on yourself and write your own story for the duration of the trip."

"I'd need a frontal lobotomy to think that was a good idea."

"But it is! Look, I never imagined that I'd be 'playing' the boyfriend of a customer in a wine shop and I'm sure you didn't think your magnum opus would be the company's health and safety manual, but here we are...at the bottom of another bottle of the rancid Rosé..." Dean held the dregs of a bottle up to the light like a scientist with an experiment.

"Perhaps that's a cue for us to call it a night. I'll sleep on it," I said, hoisting myself up with some difficulty.

"Can I sleep with you?" Dean stretched out lazily on the sofa and I tensed up and suddenly felt very sober - he was taking this pretend boyfriend thing very seriously.

"That came out wrong...I mean can I sleep on the sofa. I don't fancy my chances on the night bus in this state."

Neither did I - I wasn't even sure if he knew where he was anymore, never mind where he lived. I reckoned the chances were about even that he would accidentally get on a sleeper bus to Birmingham instead of the No.16 to Colinton.

"You can have the sofa. I'm going to attempt to find my bedroom. I may be some time."

Chapter 7

Morning came and I felt the dreadful weight of the Rosé across my forehead. I was indeed sorry for drinking it. I heard a wretched groan from the living room and remembered that Dean had stayed over. Almost the entire evening flashed through my mind as if on fast-forward, and I too groaned. What had I got myself into? There was no way to delicately extricate myself from this situation, just as there was no way to get out of bed with my dignity intact. I rolled towards the edge of the bed, each movement making my head feel like it was a Chernobyl snow globe.

After sitting in a foetal position for only a few minutes, I felt well enough to stand up and slowly approach the living room. I could hear signs of life - if you can call them that, they really sounded more like death, the odd rattling breath and groan.

"That fucking Rosé."

I nodded gingerly in agreement. Dean had managed to sit up on the sofa and seemed to be in the brace position now.

"Let's look on the bright side - thankfully it's not too bright for our hungover eyes - at least you can tell customers what the I'm Sorry Rosé tastes like."

"Regret and methamphetamines, with an aftertaste of nuclear apocalypse."

I snorted, but it hurt my inflamed sinuses too much and it turned into an 'ow'.

"I should probably get going, I think I was supposed to open the store an hour ago."

He arose from his seat slowly unfurling, like those diagrams of evolution from Neanderthal to modern man.

"We should do it again sometime with better wine. Especially if we are going to blag our way through that weekend as if we actually know each other."

Dean almost raised an eyebrow in surprise, but the Rosé was still clearly having a lingering paralytic effect on his facial muscles. Even I was surprised by my decision - perhaps I was still drunk.

"Ok," he said with a weak little smile. "Ok," the smile grew a little. "I want you to know it sounds fun, but the Rosé has left me incapable of expressing emotions with my face, ok?" He held my shoulders and nodded, whether this was to affirm his point or because he needed something to prop himself against on the way to the door, we will never know.

Chapter 8

Next week I went to the wine shop at the usual time and, if I wasn't mistaken, Dean still had a tinge of green about him, it might have been the reflection of the bottles he was carrying, but I couldn't be sure. I too felt a little green, a little too green for the whole situation. Normally, I struggled to convincingly tell Jehovah's Witnesses that I was 'in a rush', how was I going to manage a whole weekend of intricate romance fantasy with a random man, of whom the only information I had on him was that he let me buy wine without passing comment on the frequency or volume?

I looked at a wine label studiously but realised after a few minutes that I hadn't actually read anything. I was even holding Chardonnay, which I had a long-running feud with, most of which involved me violently expelling cheap bottles of it during my student years. "I don't think I can do this," I said finally.

"I know you don't like Chardonnay, but that is a bit dramatic," said Dean.

"No, I mean this plan we had. I just have a feeling of impending doom. It's like in a sitcom when the characters come up with some half-arsed plan that is inevitably going to go wrong and you get stressed out just watching them. I come out in a rash and everything."

"I'm pretty sure it's meant to be funny. It's kind of in the name too - situation comedy, you know?"

"Well, I don't find them funny! I just spend the whole episode developing anxiety rashes as it marches towards the inevitable crap conclusion. I can't do a whole weekend - I'll end up looking like the Singing Detective by the end of it."

"We can get you some cream from the chemist and I can offer to rub it on you - it will seem very nice and romantic and only help us with the ruse."

"Rubbing eczema cream on is romantic? I don't think there is enough I'm Sorry Rosé in the world to make that so."

"I actually think it's probably caused a few skin conditions."

Now that I thought about it, I actually had a stubborn patch of dry skin on my chin since the night of the dreaded Rosé. I didn't have much time to consider that state of my epidermis though, because, as, reliable as ever, we were interrupted by a phone call from Harriet.

"Hello?"

"What's up? You sound like I did when I realised those builders had botched my bathroom."

"Yes, well something is certainly botched, but it is not my bathroom."

"Oh no - please don't tell me that it is a kitchen?! Email Watchdog right away!"

"No, it just seemed like Dean and I might not be able to make it after all, but I've had a look at our schedules and we will make it work. It will be so fun to have the old gang together again. Ok-thanks-bye." The words left my mouth and I thought I'd feel instant anxiety and regret, but I didn't. Our little exchange about skin conditions had made me consider that the weekend away could be, well, fun, in a strange sort of way. I extended my free hand for a fist-bump from Dean as I put the phone back in my pocket, and he didn't leave me hanging.

If I wasn't mistaken, Dean didn't look quite as green now, and I didn't feel it, either.

"Well, what are you waiting for, pour me a glass of the wine of the week!"

"No."

We were in a wine shop. He was a purveyor of wine. I was hoping 'No' wine was the latest madcap marketing ploy from head office.

"No?"

"Well, you can have one if you want, but we're going for dinner in a few minutes, so you'll have to make it quick."

I looked into my empty wine glass as if it would provide the answer to 'what the fuck was going on' – but no luck. I decided to vocalise - that's what emotionally healthy adults do – "What the fuck is going on, Dean?"

"We're going for dinner, Sam," he said in the same tone as a quiz contestant confidently delivering their answer. "My shift finishes in 10 minutes. I'm hungry, you're probably hungry, you've not been to Marvellous Mahal yet. So let's get some food."

"But...but...It's Friday night."

"People generally go out on Friday night." Now the tone was explaining a rainbow to a small child.

"It's not part of my routine," I squirmed.

"You'll enjoy it, I promise. I'll get us a window by the bins so you can see the foxes go through them, it's supposed to be hilarious."

This genuinely made the option more palatable.

"Foxes?"

"Yes – two of them and they frolic a lot."

"But where are we going, exactly?" I asked, still not totally convinced.

"You'll see," said Dean, starting to cash up for the night.

Chapter 9

We walked away from the wine shop and towards the docks, where all the coolest bars were. It was in the opposite direction of my flat and I could feel my legs unwillingly stomping along, like a horse about to bolt. I just wanted to be in my pyjamas watching a Brat Pack movie, not having to pretend I was a normal adult for another two whole hours. Since Dean wouldn't tell me where we were going, I hadn't even had a chance to check the menu online before we went. I wondered what it would be like to be carefree enough to just turn up at a restaurant or pub without deliberating over your food choice at least three days in advance. Now it was time to find out exactly what that would feel like, in a sense. However, dread and spontaneous skin rashes probably didn't feature in most people's responses.

"Try not to look like you're enjoying yourself too much," Dean prodded as we walked along by the river that led to the docks. "People might not think I've kidnapped you then, and I'll never stand a chance at getting my own Wikipedia page."

"Fine, I'll practice mouthing 'help me' in the bathroom before we order," I swiped back.

"See, we're already like a couple and we've not even had our first 'date' yet - we are viciously seething at each other in public!"

We came to a stop at the end of the street, just before the big imposing gates of the commercial port.

"Tada!" said Dean.

"Are we going to join the merchant navy? Was that your big surprise?" I said, looking round for some sort of sign of food.

"No, we're going here for dinner," said Dean, jerking his thumb in the direction at a giant black floating object behind us; it had the outline of a bloated dead whale and the shell of an unexploded bomb.

"What even is it?"

"It's an old submarine that has been converted into a restaurant. It's called Down Below. It just opened last week and Divine Drinks supplies the wine, so they did a favour and squeezed us in."

"Oh my God," I said, taking a few steps closer to get a better look. "This is painfully hipster, even for Beath."

"Give it a chance," said Dean, beckoning me towards what was a set of steps up to the moored vessel.

"It doesn't go underwater or anything, does it?" I asked, nervously edging closer.

"No! Not since the late '70s, at least," said Dean, striding ahead

A girl with a nose ring in a military-style khaki dress greeted us at the top of the stairs. "Welcome to Down Below," she said in a bored drawl, "where you can live the high life."

"I have a reservation, Dean Malone?" he said, looking around eagerly at the metal innards of the ship.

"Ugh," she said, checking the tablet in front of her for our reservation.

"Dean! I'm so glad you came!" boomed a voice behind her. A round middle-aged man with a mid-life crisis goatee strode out from the bowels of the ship. He waved a captain's hat in greeting and proudly put it back on his head. The girl muttered something about taking her break and stalked off.

"Bobby!" said Dean, extending his hand to the man, who took it and shook it with the ferocity of a possessed Brian Blessed.

When Dean gingerly took his arm back, he explained, "This is Bobby McPhee. He owns some of the best restaurants in Scotland and this is his latest venture."

"And who is this beautiful lady?" said Bobby, assaulting Dean with a dig in the ribs.

"I'm Sam," I said, suddenly needing to put my hair up in a ponytail, avoiding his handshake death-roll.

"Sam! Dean, you're punching!" he boomed, landing a few playful but painful-looking blows on Dean's side. Dean obligingly laughed along, but even that looked like it hurt. "Let's get you two to your table - the best on board!" Bobby declared, marching down a set of echoing metal stairs.

"The new Vermentino you recommended is going down very well with the punters, Dean," said Bobby, his voice getting tinnier as we descended into the submarine. Its walls were decorated with the graffiti tags of local artists. Bobby, who saw me looking, said, "Street art at its finest. Must support local! Even if they do try and spray paint a giant boaby in the dining room."

I gave Dean a look that said, 'is this man for real?' Dean shrugged a reluctant yes.

We arrived in the centre of the submarine and Bobby opened the door to the dining room, which had a fittingly nautical feel. The floor was a chic shade of pale blue and the walls a navy colour, draped with artful tangles of thick rope. Through the portals, you could see the city lights twinkling on the water.

"I would love to dine with you both tonight," said Bobby, and both Dean and I tensed. "But I am entertaining a lassie myself this evening," we breathed a sigh of relief, but also one of pity for the poor woman. "I will leave you in the hands of my capable staff."

Another bored but beautiful young woman pointed us in the vague direction of an empty table. It was right by one of the portals, and we could see a few stragglers hurrying along the water's edge, going home for the weekend. What was in store for them? Was it Brat Pack films alone, or was it dinner dates with strange men as part of some convoluted plan to look like a socially successful human being?

Our bored waitress slung a couple of menus on our table. From my angle, I saw her slip behind the bar, sit on the floor and start taking selfies.

Just then Bobby reappeared with a woman on his arm. She was probably about his age but trying to look younger in a spaghetti-strap pink dress. It was very on-trend, but probably from one of those shops that would try and make people prove they were under-25 before allowing them to buy their clothes if they could. She had a good figure and a healthy glow about her, so she got away with it, though. They walked towards our table and I buried my head in the menu.

"Melinda! This is Sam and Dean," Bobby announced. The rest of us did polite mumbled hellos. Then Bobby ripped the menu out of my hand. "Where are my manners? You shouldn't have to trouble your pretty head with thinking about what to have for dinner. I'll see to it that the kitchen sends you two only the finest grub on the menu."

I think I was too shocked by the misogyny to actually say anything. Dean mouthed 'sorry', and Melinda smiled around the room like she was on stage in a Miss World contest.

"Anyway, we must get some dinner for ourselves too," he said, guiding Melinda away in front of him. "Melinda and I are having a business dinner," he said, turning back to our table, making an unsubtle humping motion at Melinda.

"That man is disgusting!" I hissed at Dean. "How can we eat here and support his business?!"

"He's giving us it all for free because I cut him a deal on the Vermentino wine. His chef used to work in the best restaurant in Marseilles and the normal price for a meal here is £250."

"Fair enough," I said, willing to put the chauvinism aside for a good meal. Or at least until I could draw a willy on the wall of the bathroom when I went to the loo, that would really wind him up.

A platter of shiny pink shellfish arrived at our table, along with two glasses of pink champagne. We thanked yet another disinterested waitress, who said "Whatever" and stormed back to the kitchen.

We began to pick at the, admittedly, very good food. Bobby was now in full voice, the big man on campus indulging in a bit of dinner theatre.

"Melinda, you are in the wellness industry, is that correct?"

"Yes I am Bobby," she said, batting her eyelashes almost as much as if a pigeon had just flown at her.

"I guess you are a natural. You do look very well indeed," he said with a waggle of his eyebrows. I just about managed to suppress a gag. "I'm embarrassed for him," muttered Dean into his champagne.

"You're too kind, Bobby! But it is a new wellness venture that I wanted to talk to you about," said Melinda. "I think Down Below would be the perfect venue for it." I wondered how she was managing to put up with Bobby's skin-crawling routine. Vodka? Prescription medication? Both?

"Tell me more, my sweet Melinda," Bobby said, laughing at his own wordplay. No one else did. "I plan to convert some space onboard into boutique rooms and a small wellness centre could be the perfect complement."

"I am so glad to hear that, although, I must admit, not everyone is open to alternative therapies. Is that something you believe in, Bobby?" said Melinda. I had a feeling Bobby would believe in UFOs if it meant he stood a chance with a beautiful woman.

"Of course!" he declared, in between sloppy mouthfuls of crayfish.

"I am so pleased to hear that. Colonic hydrotherapy is very misunderstood," said Melinda, daintily extracting meat from a lobster shell.

Dean and I looked at each other, our eyes bulging as if we ourselves had just been subjected to colonic hydrotherapy.

"C-c-colonic hydrotherapy, you say?" said Bobby, turning an ashen shade.

"Yes. It is a very spiritual experience," said Melinda. I wondered what else she considered a spiritual experience. A Brazilian bikini wax? Food poisoning?

"Oh I er, um, yes, well," said Bobby, pushing a slice of smoked salmon around his plate.

"Oh dear, Bobby, I've put you on the spot," said Melinda, reaching across the table and placing a hand on Bobby's arm. His eyes lit up. "I don't expect you to make a decision tonight, and you have already been so generous with this beautiful meal."

"Well, I'll certainly have a think-"

"I know!" said Melinda, her arms flying up into the air. "You must experience it for yourself. It's the least I can do to thank you for your incredible hospitality." I could think of a few things Bobby might prefer as a thank you, including a firing squad. "It would bring us even closer together," she said, running her finger around the rim of her glass. Bobby genuinely considered it for a second.

"Melinda, that's very kind of you but-" stammered Bobby.

"We can go right now! I run it out the back of my van, it's in the car park. It's a very auspicious time for the procedure too, Mercury is in retrograde," said Melinda, already getting up from the table.

"Well, I..." said Bobby as she slipped her arm through his and began to guide him out of the restaurant.

Bobby walked past our table with the resignation of a condemned man. He gave us a helpless shrug as Melinda pulled him along. "You've got to try everything once," he explained.

"Do you think he is really going to do it?" I gasped, once they were safely out of earshot.

"I'm trying not to think about it," said Dean, poking an oyster on his plate. "Urgh, it's no use, I can't eat after that chat."

"Let's get out of here before someone tries to give us a colonoscopy or something," I said as we stood up from the table.

Outside the submarine, we saw Melinda's van but kept walking, uneager to find out what was going on inside.

As we walked back along the docks, I began to laugh.

"What's so funny?" asked Dean.

"Well, Melinda was right. What better place for colonic hydrotherapy than somewhere called Down Below?"

Chapter 10

Later that week, looking back in quieter moments, I found myself returning to what exactly was going on with this whole thing. And, as when you are stuck in your own mental merry-go-round with no one else to pull the brakes, I began to obsess over what ulterior motives Dean could have for doing this. I had no illusions that he was nice to me in the shop as I probably paid for the majority of his salary, but why was he going to all this effort? It was really taking after sales care too far. Lying in bed at night, I would walk down the dark and winding pathways of my imagination - was he a long-lost brother with a grudge? Perhaps he was hired by Harriet for the humiliation - he did say he had thespian aspirations, after all.

Or were we really becoming friends? We seemed to have a similar sense of humour and have a good time together. While the least dramatic, this option was probably the most normal outcome. Maybe this was how you made friends as an adult, without the ready-made social scene of university life. That was probably it, I would think, putting the more ridiculous scenarios out of my head.

However, I couldn't shake the feeling of unease completely. In situations like this, most people would speak to an old friend to put their mind at ease, but I knew I didn't have that option. Someone from their university days who knows them better than anyone else. I couldn't risk something getting back to Harriet though, inadvertently or not. Work 'friends' were not really an option either - I remember the time they judged me for saying I didn't watch Big Brother, so trying to explain that I was apparently living in a complicated farce culled from an episode of Frasier was unlikely to go down well.

So, I turned not to a priest or, what is probably quite advisable in my case, a therapist, but to my masseuse. To the uneducated, she was a delicate little Thai woman, but she pounced on clients two or three times her size with a passion and brutish force more often seen on a rugby pitch.

When you first entered her massage parlour, you were usually greeted by wafting aromas of jasmine and fragrant oils, a benevolent looking Buddha statue and tinkling traditional music. Then June or another masseuse would appear in semi-traditional garb, normally 'I went on my Gap Year to Thailand' elephant patterned harem pants and a saree-style top. She even had a Thai Ridgeback dog, named Leni, an imposing, gargoyle of a beast that looked like it should be standing outside a rough nightclub with its arms folded, not lolling on a waiting room sofa.

I had started going to June's massage parlour a couple of years ago after developing a sore neck from sitting at my desk all day. The results were good so I made it a regular thing. June was of indeterminate age and you never knew very much about her from the average massage session - she simply bowed when you paid and occasionally asked 'you like?' and 'too hard?' The confirmation emails were even written in a charmingly broken English that gave the whole thing an extra air of authenticity to the average white client, which was most of us.

That was until I turned up a little early for my appointment one day a year or so ago to find the door slightly ajar and barking and banging coming from inside.

"I need to get in the cash register, you useless cretin!"

My active imagination once again sprang into action - a robbery was clearly in progress. June had been good to me and respected my need not to make conversation and had never instructed Leni to savage me, as she so easily could, so I decided, with some trepidation, that I must save her from these no good thieves - even if they did have some good insults.

In front of me stood a hooded figure towering over Leni, who was cowering, even though all his muscles were still rippling. I thought they weren't the typical local thug - velour joggers were a bold choice for your average career criminal, as was the hoodie, which had 'grumpy but gorgeous' emblazoned in rhinestones.

"It's you! I mean, ah, Miss Sam! You early!"

"'Useless cretin'?'" This was not the charmingly broken English that was usually trotted out at the massage parlour.

"What did you expect? I've lived here for 25 years!" sighed June as she shooed Leni away from the reception desk.

"Of course, that's a good point," I admitted, but was still a little confused as to what was going on.

"Nobody wants someone who speaks better English than them massaging them. They want a little Thai lady fresh off the boat. I believe it's what Edward Said referred to as the 'exotic other'."

"The exotic other?"

"Surprise! I've got a Masters in Cultural Studies. What do you think all the massage money went on?"

"Next you will be telling me 'Leni' is short for Lenin and you advocate a Marxist approach to sociological theories."

"So what if I do?"

From then on, June and I had become good friends. Sometimes I would stop in on my way home from work with a bottle of wine from Divine Drinks and we would talk about our days, or June would bring a DVD round of some classic of Socialist cinema she would insist I have to watch, or we would take Leni for a walk around Arthur's Seat.

She always had good advice, even if it always seemed to somehow come back to seizing the means of production. So, I decided to stop in and get her perspective on the situation I found myself in.

We had arranged to have a glass of wine after work that week, so it seemed like the ideal time to ask her. As usual, I would bring around a bottle to her shop and we would stretch out on her huge waiting room sofa and chew the fat.

I arrived about 5.30pm to find a woman about my age with blonde dreadlocks and a distinct scent of bad local cannabis slipping on her sandals in the reception area. I picked a perch on the far end of the sofa and did that awkward half-smile everyone does in the confines of a public space. She returned the greeting with the beaming, blissed-out smile of the freshly massaged. I turned and gazed straight ahead at the collection of buddha figurines and statues exhibited in her window.

Thankfully, June padded out from the massage room and saved me from having to attempt conversation.

"You like?" she asked her dreadlocked customer with a meek nod.

"It was very good," the woman said at a volume Brits reserve for the deaf and foreigners.

"I glad," a huge smile appeared on June's face. "£55, please."

"It's so charming that she only takes cash, she's so cute," she said to me. "It's just like being back in Thailand."

Yes, having locals put on a fantasy of exoticism for you. How perceptive, I thought, catching June's twitching eye.

"Ok, bye bye now," said June, receiving the money with a bow.

The woman ambled out the shop to inflict herself on someone else. June waved at her through the window. "What an absolute moron," she said through clenched teeth.

"I got that vibe," I said, stretching out on the sofa.

June went over to the till and slipped the takings in. "She spent the entire massage prattling on about how spiritual it was to hold a baby tiger at some roadside zoo near Phuket. It made me remember why I came here in the first place, to avoid Brits abroad, but it turns out they can be just as bad on their home soil." June took two wine glasses out from behind the counter and I pulled the bottle out of my bag.

"I've been booked solid all day," she said, taking the bottle from me and plunging a corkscrew into it. "Thanks for bringing some vino over. I haven't had a chance to pee all day, let alone nip out to the shops. Which reminds me, I better go to the loo now before I get one of those camel humps." June quickly poured a couple of glasses with a slightly pained expression, obviously trying not to think too much about flowing liquid.

"Where did you pick the wine up? Divine Drinks?" she called as she passed me a glass.

"Yeah, I picked it up on Friday. I've actually got some gossip for you," I said, trying to laugh casually. "It's a funny story, you'll never believe it-"

"Hold that thought, because I can't hold this in any longer," said June, shuffling at speed towards the loo. I leaned over to the speakers her phone was plugged into and changed the soundtrack from massage muzak to one of her punk rock playlists.

"Ugh, thank you, Sam. I can only listen to so much pan pipe music before I cave someone's head in with one of my giant Buddha statues," June said, appearing back in the reception with a relieved look on her face. "Cheers!" she said, taking a slug of the wine and falling back in her chair. "So, what's the gossip, then?"

"Like I said, it's a funny story," I said, bringing the glass of wine to my lips like it was a microphone and I was a stand-up comedian.

"Are you sure? Because I often marvel at how many times my clients profess that and it absolutely is not a funny story." Leni waddled out of the backroom and plonked himself on top of June's lap like a lap dog, not the 80-pound beast he was. June bore it with remarkable fortitude though, patting his back with one hand and sipping wine with the other.

"Oh, I think you'll be amused," I laughed, but I felt like I too had a massive dog on my chest now. The whole situation was really getting embarrassing, not funny for me.

"It was something to do with Divine Drinks, right?" said June, hugging Leni close.

"Yeah, you've been in there a few times, right?"

"Yes, especially after a long day of hearing how wonderful it is to pet a drugged-up baby tiger or ride an abused elephant in Thailand," she said.

"Have you ever met the younger guy who works there?" I asked, putting a lot of effort into nonchalantly swirling my glass.

"I think so," said June. "Stubble? Passable looks?"

I nodded. "Yes, I think we are talking about the same person."

"Are you two dating?" June asked, Leni abruptly awakening as she jiggled in her seat.

"This is exciting, you've not been out with anyone in a while."

"Thank you for the reminder, June, but no, we are not dating. Well, not really."

“Not really? Is it a no-strings attached thing? There’s nothing wrong with that. It’s all good practice, isn’t it? They say sex is like riding a bike, but it is a bit embarrassing if you fall off doing either,” she said with a wicked wink.

“Again, thank you for the concern, but it’s not that either. I’ve got myself into a bit of a situation with Harriet from uni.”

“Is that the one who is a bit stuck up now?”

“Yeah, well, I was at Divine Drinks and she called about our alumni reunion. Dean answered my phone, I suppose for a bit of a laugh, and, basically, she now thinks we are a couple and now we have to go to the reunion together.”

“Well, I must say, Sam, this is much better gossip than I normally get in here,” June said, raising her glass to me. “One time I had to pretend to be interested in someone’s search for a chiropodist courageous enough to try and cut their fungal nail.”

“My condolences.”

“But this almost makes up for that traumatic time,” June said, pouring more wine into her glass. “Dean has served me a couple of times. He is a bit of a snack, isn’t he? And not completely dead from the neck up; we’ve discussed Peter Brook’s approach to theatre and its influence on 1980s music videos.”

I wasn’t sure how to respond to that, just as I wasn’t sure how to respond to anything at the moment. Of course June used more current slang than me, despite being 40. She probably accidentally got a PhD in Theatre Studies at some point too.

“He says he is doing it to help me out and we are sort of becoming friends. We even went out for dinner the other night.”

“What’s the big deal? Maybe it could become something more?” June shrugged.

“I don’t know. I just can’t shake the feeling that it’s all an act. He knows how to play a part. One night, he is a theatre aficionado with you, the next, he is making fun of colonic hydrotherapy with me.”

“I’m not even going to touch that one,” said June. “But I think you are forgetting something. How did you and I become friends?”

"I met you here?" I said, sitting in the very same room where I had graduated from customer to friend.

"Exactly. And now we are, like, total BFFs!" June said in her best American teenager voice.

"True! But I'm just not sure about the whole thing with Dean," I said, snuggling into the marshmallow sofa, wishing I could just hibernate in it for a few months and skip the whole thing.

"Why not?"

"Why not?" I repeated, confused.

"You Brits are so fond of that phrase. 'Let's get black-out drunk.' 'Why not?' 'Let's have another family-sized pack of biscuits each'.' 'Why not?' 'Let's impersonate someone's significant other at a reunion?"

"Why not?"

"You see where I am going with this," June said, grabbing Leni's lead - wine o'clock was coming to an end and it was almost time for walkies. "It's not just a British thing, though. I remember thinking 'why not?' about moving to this country 25 years ago, and it didn't turn out too badly for me. I mean, I have a work persona, but doesn't everyone? I have a nice house, a Masters degree and my lovely little Leni," she said, receiving a massive lick from the adoring Leni.

"So, you're saying 'why not?' can lead to good things?" I said, draining my glass. I gathered my things and headed for the door with June and Leni.

"Why not?" said June with an infuriating giggle as we walked out the shop. She locked the door and I pulled down the shutters. I had my uses, being quite a bit taller than her.

Our conversation was disturbed by Leni catching sight of a poodle sashaying by, which caused June to be dragged across the street by him. I waved goodbye and started to make my own way home. Perhaps June was on to something with the theory of Why Not, I thought. There was only one way to find out. I mean, why not?

Chapter 11

If I was really going to do this, then I would need an ally from St Fillan's to keep up the ruse. Luckily, I knew just the man for the job: Paxton. We had worked on the student newspaper together. Well, he didn't really 'work', he just rocked up often enough that his newspaper tycoon father kept sending his incredibly generous allowance from the States. He came from such a privileged world that it was obscene, or it would be if he wasn't so down to earth, as happy in an old man pub as a private member's club. He was kind of like a Kennedy brother, without the curse or political ambition and added nudity and Prosecco.

I scheduled a video call with him to get him up to speed. "Are you going to the reunion?" I tried to ask breezily, but it came out with a distinctly strangled quality. I was really pinning a lot of hope on him going, the prospect of him not being there was making me nervous.

"Am I going to the reunion? Is the Pope Catholic? Is my father still threatening to disinherit me? It's one of life's inevitabilities, like birth, death and taxes," said Paxton. I could have done without the monologue, but I was relieved he was going.

I could see that Paxton was in his Maine pied-à-terre, an old family farmhouse that was straight out of an interior design magazine. Literally, it had been in quite a few publications. Everything was a tasteful shade of duck egg blue, with the odd splash of Little Women rustic charm; a wrought iron fireplace here, a vintage handwoven rug there. This was Paxton though, so it wasn't totally tasteful; there were old framed Playboys all the way up the staircase and he had mounted his St Fillan's hoodie above the fireplace (a St Fillan's tradition was to write the most obscene things possible on graduate's hoodies, and Paxton's made the front page of a right-wing tabloid).

I knew it was his Maine home because Harriet and I had visited him one summer after we graduated. It must have only been one or two years later; it was that time when you have started earning money but don't realise you are actually poor yet. Now, with my tupperware lunches and supermarket wardrobe, I was well and truly aware that my best opportunity to see Paxton would be to get him back across the Atlantic. Plus, I really needed him to help Dean and me. First of all, he was rich and bored, so usually up for any hairbrained scheme. Second of all, despite, or perhaps because, he was the sort of guy who played golf with politicians at the weekend and got invited to the birthday parties of Hollywood brats, he could be trusted to be discreet - when he felt like it.

"You're going too?" he asked me. "I thought you said, what was it, that you would rather boil and eat your own face?"

"Harriet is making me. Sort of."

"How is Harriet? Still married to what's-his-name?" called Paxton, who was now mixing himself a martini in the kitchen.

"His name's Allan. You know it is, you shared a flat with him for a year!" I took a sip of off-brand fruit tea from my St Fillan's mug.

"Sam, don't act so righteous," he said in between cocktail shakes. "We both know he was so unmemorable his own parents forgot to pick him up one summer."

I stifled a snort. "I'm sure that was just a cruel rumour." I waved Lily away from this week's pasta. The call had interrupted me dividing it up into batches for lunch at work.

"I was there! It was not a rumour!" said Paxton, taking an incredulous sip of his freshly prepared martini.

"Well, that makes it even crueller, Paxton. And I was calling to let you in on a secret."

"A secret? Colour me intrigued," he said, stroking new sideburns that would have looked more fitting on his newspaper magnate great grandfather. "I will be the soul of discretion, my dear lady."

"Thank you, kind sir." In my own kitchen, I was fixing the plastic lid on top of Wednesday's pasta.

"Well, tell me! I am on tenterhooks, you saucy wench."

"Since you asked so nicely," I said, dispatching Wednesday's pasta to the fridge.

"Yes? Come on, I'm bored. My Porsche is in the shop and the nearest bar is 10 miles away," he whined.

"Ok," I huffed theatrically. "To cut a long story short, Harriet thinks this guy who answered my phone and spoke to her is my boyfriend, which he most definitely isn't."

"So far, so juicy. Continue," said Paxton.

"Anyway, the guy, Dean, fell into one of Harriet's little verbal traps and now we are going to have to go to the reunion together."

Paxton let out a guffaw so hearty that I could have probably heard it across the Atlantic without the aid of the internet.

"Yes, yes, it's very amusing. Get it out of your system," I said through gritted teeth.

The laughter continued.

"That's it, let it all out. I'm going to need you to act cool at the reunion and help us out."

Paxton had now stopped shaking with laughter enough that he could drink his martini without any spillages.

"Say no more. This is going to be hilarious. In fact, it already is. Sam, I really have to go now. I am going riding with the Senator from next door at 4 o'clock and I haven't even got my jodhpurs on yet. But I can't wait to see you and this Dean in a few weeks!"

"Have fun, Paxton," I said, almost feeling the privilege radiate through the screen.

"I always do!" he said as he hung up.

Chapter 12

The following Monday, a message popped up on my phone:

> Harriet:
>
> Why are there no photos of Dean? I'm on your Facebook page and can't see a thing.

It stared at me, as unanswerable as an exam question that I hadn't prepared for. I knew I was going to have to cheat to answer it, so I screenshotted it and sent it to Dean.

The reply was a stream of selfies taken around the wine shop with a gradually decreasing resemblance to reality. First there was Dean in a passport-style pose, then Dean with a unicorn filter over his face at the till, then peering through a display of bottles and finally with a cardboard box over his head with two eyeholes cut out.

> Sam:
>
> Thank you Annie Leibovitz - but I think we are going to need photos together. Harriet is a known social media stalker.

This was followed by a photo of him and what appeared to be a woman in her 80s in Divine Drinks – it was hard to tell as he had put an emoji with loveheart eyes over her face; I was basing this purely on the scoliosis, shawl and walking stick.

> Dean:
>
> Do you think she'd believe this was you?

I replied with an eye-roll emoji.

Then came the same set of pictures with me hastily copied and pasted in from an old holiday album he had obviously found on my Facebook page. I hadn't looked at the thing in years and I must have forgotten to make the album private back in the day. At the very least, Harriet would surely wonder why I was wearing a 'Malaga 2009' t-shirt in all these snaps.

Sam:
As convincing as these are, I think we are going to have to put a bit more work in. Holidays, birthday parties, meals out, obnoxious selfies for no obvious reason - the standard basic bitch couple fare.

Dean:
True. I see nothing else on my feed, although it makes me want to put myself out of my misery with a bottle of wine to the head.

Sam:
It's totally false but that's what real relationships are these days.

The dots appeared on the screen for a few seconds, followed only by the word:

Dean:
Deep

Dean:
How are we going to do it?

I had an idea.

That night on the way home from work, I knocked on June's shop door just as she was cashing up for the day. She waved me in with one hand as she counted cash with the other. I knew she had been roped into photographing her niece's Sweet Sixteen, and the photos weren't half-bad. She had even done a pretty good job at photoshopping out all the acne, which was so prevalent it appeared contagious in the untouched originals. I reckoned that with the promise of a free bottle of Divine Drinks' finest botanical gin, she might be persuaded to get behind the lens again.

"I did a semester in Advanced Photography back in the day, actually. I wouldn't mind updating my portfolio too. I can only do so much with those Sweet Sixteen ones," June said, concentrating on the money in front of her.

"So, you'll do it?"

"If it is on a Tuesday during the day. It's slow here then," June said, looking past me to her collection of buddhas in the window. She just couldn't leave the shop without them looking perfect. She got up and adjusted one of them to face the sun a little and frowned, turning it back to its original position.

"Thank you June!! I don't know why you're helping me out, but I won't forget it."

June was still engrossed in her Buddha arrangement, though. The Buddha in question wasn't like the rest, which were of a classic, uniform red resin, all in peaceful meditation. This one was an old, burnished bronze, and was drinking merrily from some sort of pouch.

"I really mean it, June, thank you," I tried again.

"Sorry, it's an old family heirloom an aunt insisted I have last time I was home, and I just can't find the right place for it."

"Why not stick it on eBay or give it to a charity shop?"

"Get rid of it? Never. I've always got to help people - inanimate or not" said June, giving the figurine a comforting pat. "What is the appropriate behaviour for a man or a woman in the midst of this world, where each person is clinging to his piece of debris? What's the proper salutation between people as they pass each other in this flood?"

"Eh?"

"It's a Buddha quote."

"Oh," I bowed my head solemnly towards the Buddha.

"Oh, I've never been religious. My parents were atheists too. I just saw it on one of those inspirational quote memes once and liked it."

"I'm not 100% what it means, but does it, in a broader sense, mean you'll take some photos of Dean and I so that I can convince Harriet we have been a couple for a while?"

June sighed wearily and readjusted the Buddha. "Yes. Meet me outside the shop at 10am on Tuesday," she said.

Time to fake a dentist appointment at work, I thought. Perhaps make it believable and mention a loose filling on Monday.

"Thank you June, I don't know how I'll ever repay you for all this. Gin will hopefully be a good start, though" I couldn't help it, I bowed again to the Buddha, and, pleasantries completed, I turned to leave, but then a pang of dread seized me. Normally, I only got these on Sunday when I thought about going back to work the next day.

How was I going to do all this without June? I asked myself as I looked at the empty street. I always came to her for advice and help, for everything from niggling back pain to advanced photographic deception, apparently. I would need moral support in St Fillan's to keep up this charade. Harriet would delight in any minor misstep, and I was sure she wouldn't be the only one. Who really goes to a reunion anyway, unless it is to get fresh dirt on your oldest friends? Does anyone really care that so-and-so is now Head of Planning at the local council, or are they waiting for them to have six glasses of wine and sob about how they were jilted at the altar at their Barbados beach wedding?

I was determined not to end up in a terrible post-reunion folk tale like that.

"June?"

"Is the door stuck?"

I realised I had been standing there a while and jumped out the way for her. She gave it a good pull and it flew open.

"Seems fine to me," she said, buttoning up her denim jacket. Her back was turned to me now, and I could see had sewn on a new patch, a guitar design with 'This machine kills fascists' written on it.

"Nice new patch," I said, trying to screw up enough courage to ask her to come to St Fillan's with me.

"Come on, come on! If I don't get home in 15 minutes, Leni will do a protest poo on my Persian rug," she said, shooing me out the shop.

She locked up in record time and began to speed walk towards the bus stop. I tagged along too, even though my flat was only a 5-minute walk in the other direction.

"Hang on, shouldn't you head the other way?" she asked as we reached the bus shelter.

June's bus was hurtling down the street, time was running out.

"I actually have one more favour to ask," I blurted out.

"Well, make it quick!" June was counting out her fare now.

"Come to the reunion with me," I said. As the words left my mouth, I wished the ground would swallow me up. June had much better things to do with her time, like studying for her next Masters degree or perfecting her photography portfolio.

"Come to the reunion? But I didn't go there the first-time round," she laughed, but she didn't seem totally averse to the idea either. Her bus was drawing up though and I was running out of time. I decided to sweeten the deal.

"All expenses paid. I'll even throw in a day pass to the Farquhar Spa Hotel. You know it's one of the best around. Treat yourself to a massage for a change and do some recon for your shop?"

The bus doors opened with a hydraulic sigh and June stepped on and handed over her money to the driver. Her back to me, I wondered if there was space for a St Fillan's patch on her jacket.

She turned back to answer. As she opened her mouth, the doors snapped shut and the bus took off down the street as if it was being pursued in a high-speed chase.

I stood there for a few seconds, wondering if this was some sort of divine intervention to spare June from hurting my feelings. The bus to Haymarket was notoriously late and always got stuck in roadworks for the trams, so it was a miracle it had made its way down the walk so hastily.

Then I felt my phone vibrate in my pocket.

> Comrade June:
>
> What was up with that bus?! And OK, I will come to the reunion. I can bring down that fancy corporate spa from the inside with the day pass;)

I wrote back 'Thank you', followed by about a thousand love hearts.

Comrade June:

My car will be out the shop next week, I can drive us all up. I've never been to St Fillan's, and, from what you've told me, I might finally be able to eat the rich there. All I ask (apart from the spa pass obvs) is that I get to watch the hilarity ensue when you two pretend to be love's young dream!

I sent her a thumbs up, but really I was cringing at the 'love's young dream' bit.

9.55am the next Tuesday I found Dean outside the massage shop, shoulders hunched against the cold and sunglasses firmly over his eyes. A stuffed 'Bag for Life' was having its name put the test as he wrung it in his hands.

"Are you going for the mid-morning drug deal look?"

"Very funny. The shop only ever opens at 12 so this is an ungodly early hour for me. Direct sunlight at this time is traumatic. I feel like I am going to melt like that Nazi in Indiana Jones."

"I'll tell June not to use the flash then, it could finish you off."

"The sweet embrace of death might be welcome, actually."

"What's in the bag?"

"The cognitive processes are still shuddering into gear, I don't remember what I threw in this thing last night," Dean shifted his sunglasses for a better look. "Let's see - scarf, straw hat, a giant pumpkin hat, sparklers."

I nodded approvingly. We had decided to collect together a few props for our photos to simulate the different seasons and this clearly had us covered through spring, summer, Halloween and Guy Fawkes' night/New Year. Even the sunglasses could be put to good use in completing our summer scene.

"What about you?"

I patted my rucksack, "I've got it in the bag," I winked and snorted to myself. Then considered that the reason I was having to stage a relationship was probably something to do with awful puns and poor sinus control.

The shutter behind us snapped open and this time I snorted like a startled pig and gave up any last sense of dignity that had been circling the drain.

"Come in!" commanded June. "This way!" We ducked under the shutter and June marched us through to Massage Room 2, despite both of us stomping about like unwilling war elephants.

A wave of heat hit us, as did an interrogation-like bright light when June opened the door. After our senses began to adjust to the onslaught, it became clear that the floor below us was uneven and we were apparently sinking. So this is what it came to, I thought, killed by some crazed massage therapist in her torture chamber of quicksand and her Abu Ghraib hand-me-downs. This was the last time I would trust a mysterious Marxist massage lady, I vowed.

My eyes began to focus more and I could make out the Thai beach scene that I had seen so many times before on the far wall of the treatment room. Then came the realisation that all the heat was coming from a giant photographer's lighting rig crammed into the corner of the compact room. Finally, I looked down to see just plain old sand at my feet, not the murderous quicksand my mind had conjured up. I had to give it to June, the whole thing almost looked like a snapshot of a Thai resort.

"I'm impressed."

"Oh yes!" chimed in Dean agreeably, as if he was viewing a house for sale. He had still to be introduced properly to June in this new context; he had clearly defaulted to pleasant stranger mode, despite 'WTF' flickering into his eyes like cherries on a slot machine.

"Welcome to Ko Samui!" June proclaimed with a witchy laugh, arms outstretched at the scene she had conjured. "Get in your beach gear, we are going to take some photos."

I am not sure if it was out of habit or not, but June then quietly shut the door just as she always did to allow a client to undress. We hastily took off our layers under the beach towels we had found lying on the floor - June had really thought of every detail. She really was earning that spa pass before we had even left town.

The whole experience felt more like a primary school trip to a swimming pool than an exotic holiday though - we had come prepared with swimsuits under our everyday clothes and shivered as we waited to be told what to do, even under the bright light. I imagined that Dean was shivering a little extra due to the realisation that he was having to pass off being in a relationship not with a woman, but actually a goose-pimpled occupant of a poultry aisle shoved into a tattered bikini found at the back of a wardrobe. Men didn't have any of this to contend with, I sniffed internally as I looked at Dean, clad in the standard issue navy blue Club 18-30 board shorts, kept warm by a sprinkling of body hair. I was just formulating a particularly vitriolic feminist rant on personal grooming when came June's obligatory knock before she entered a treatment room. "Old habits!" she laughed as she fiddled with her intimidatingly fancy camera's buttons.

"I know this is hard for British people, but try and look relaxed," said June.

We both robotically switched to 'smiling in photos' mode, much to her displeasure. June's face twisted in response. "You're all the same, you really are." We laughed, a little weakly and confused as to whether we should find that funny. "That's better! A little, anyway," June tried to hide a grimace as she looked at the picture. She snapped a few more and the UFO-like light she had installed began to warm us. Our smiles became less forced and June finally pronounced, "That will have to do. At least Brits have a reputation for being awkward, it's to be expected." With that ringing endorsement, she hauled her equipment out of the room and left us to get dressed.

We faced firmly away from each other and began to re-layer. "Is it bad I feel like I want to impress her? Each time she frowns or makes that vomity face at the camera, I feel like I am back in school trying to get a teacher to love me. You know, when you'd watch them mark an essay and any little expression had to be analysed."

"I knew you were that girl," Dean said as he pulled a sweater back on. "The grade girl. You didn't care if anyone liked you, as long as you got the grades. That's not strictly true, you wanted the teacher to like you."

I tried to formulate a retort but I felt like a ventriloquist who had lost his voice as I mouthed silent syllables. "How did you know?" I finally arrived on.

"You're doing all this," Dean gestured to the fluorescent lighting, the sand, the outfit, himself, "to impress people you don't actually like because it's what you should do."

I stood in my bikini pants looking sadly down at my jeggings, hoping they might hold a spare personality in the back pocket. Then I remembered something. "Hang on, you're the one who got me into this mess, Dean Malone!"

"Yes, that's true - technically. But look at your way of getting out of it," Dean turned around and waved at the scene. "Not that it's the worst thing in the world, you know. We all carry around our baggage, and not just in plastic bags. I wasn't exactly the coolest kid in school either."

"No?"

Dean put his hand on the door and listened for any traces of June. "Promise not to tell? Even after a bottle of I'm Sorry Rosé?"

"That stuff is beyond the mortal realm but I'll do my best."

"I was a Goth," he whispered.

Suddenly, everything was illuminated. The dark clothes, the pale skin, the weirdly encyclopaedic knowledge of 'Wines Dracula would have definitely drunk' which came out at Halloween.

"Wow, well that is definitely up there with my people-pleasing swot thing. A gothic act-or."

"They were separate endeavours!" declared Dean as he swished open the door, making a grand exit worthy of an early Bela Lugosi.

The indignance didn't last long and he couldn't help but laugh at himself. I was also going to have trouble wiping the smirk off my face in time for the next 'photoshoot'.

"If only you two could have looked like that when I was taking the photos!" said June, appearing from her office. "Oh well, can't have everything. I thought we would go to the park across the way for the rest of the pics. Try and find some flowers for a nice but slightly pathetic spring photo in overcast weather, some cheesy 'Halloween' images in the woods, set off some fireworks for that day the British celebrate torturing and burning a Catholic to death. You know, your standard cultural institutions."

We couldn't disagree with logic like that, so we dutifully followed June to the park. I admired her bravery for proudly hanging her expensive camera around her neck as she walked through the gate. Most people, even locals, only heard of the park due to its colourful appearances in the local press - Man Stabs Drone in Spice Trance, Doggers Play Fetch for Charity and Pensioner Robbed of Cane and Dignity being some of the most memorable headlines associated with it. On paper, Dean and I were probably going to be mugged and set on fire with a homemade flamethrower. I began to follow June to distract myself from the prospect.

"Stop," said Dean.

"We've got to keep going in here. It's like being a shark, keep moving or die," I hissed.

"No, I think we should get some camouflage," Dean gave a pantomime nod to the dilapidated corner shop clinging to the edge of the park.

June was busy eyeing different angles next to a park bench as I felt a tug on my arm pulling me towards the shop. Inside, we navigated crowded crisp packet displays and an overpowering yet otherwise quite indescribable odour towards the booze section at the back. It was full of obscure brands, but not in the way the wine shop was. There it was niche producers from Hungary or Lebanon with bottles dressed in chic simple labels. Here, everything was almost beyond the realms of human comprehension. Yes, the products were ostensibly in bottles and, if you had to guess, you could probably work out whether it was a spirit or a cider, but the neon, unreadable labels looked like they belonged in a top secret chemical laboratory, not out here for public consumption.

"Ah, Bat Brew," Dean said fondly. "I used to drink this in the local cemetery all the time when I was 15." I swear I saw tears in his eyes. Dean tenderly picked it off the shelf and took it to the till, handing over some pocket change in payment.

"I know it looks like there could be a few dead bodies in the park, but there is no need for us to join them - isn't it a bit extreme to resort to Bat Brew?"

"Sometimes it just calls to you," said Dean as we went back into the street.

"Does it sound like 'neepneepneepneep'?" I said, flapping my arms up and down to complete the bat impression. An intimidating looking muscle man in a grey tracksuit crossed the street to avoid us.

"Laugh all you want but I'm having my Bat Brew," he took a swig and made a face that was as scrunched up as a bat's.

"Not what you remembered?"

"I think the bloody thing must have wiped my memory. That is truly disgusting."

"I hope you don't make faces like that in my photos!" called June from a bench. "Now come over here and look happy."

We dutifully went over, Dean's eyes searching for somewhere to dispose of the Bat Brew.

"What are you looking so sad about now?" demanded June.

"I've just had my entire adolescence ruined."

"Yes, well most of us do at some point," dismissed June.

"Usually during your adolescence," I chimed in.

"Oh, please spare me the pubescent struggles of privileged white people. I've just had my breakfast," June said, clutching her stomach. "Go and stand underneath that underpass." The last words were almost said in the same tone as soldiers in films as they line people up against walls. June could see we looked doubtful. She began to cackle. "You're in a park filled with junkies and jakies and you're scared of me? I want you to stand over there because it is 12.30pm and it needs to be night-time for your Guy Fawkes and New Year's moments." It did sound plausible, I had to admit.

"Stand over there by that shopping trolley," said June, pointing to the dingiest corner of the underpass. We shuffled over, our steps echoing alongside the steady drip of water that every underpass seems to have. June handed us both a sparkler, but it took a few goes for each one to light in the dank environment. As someone who finds the 'big light' in the living room overwhelming, I didn't cope too well in this scenario. As the stick hissed and hurled its immolating self about the underpass, I blinked uncontrollably and held it at arm's length, suddenly remembering the overdramatic government adverts of my youth in which someone usually had their face burnt off by a seemingly innocuous firework.

June, too exhausted to have a strong reaction to the latest fuck up, kept snapping away. "What's wrong?" asked Dean through gritted teeth, somehow managing to hold a smile for the camera. "I can't deal with this!" I whimpered as I launched the sparkler into a murky puddle.

"Nobody ever died from a sparkler!" he laughed. I made a mental note to fact-check that when I got home. Suddenly I was very much over this whole photoshoot idea. What would I have to remember this day by? Goose-pimpled bikini pics and a selection of underpass images in which I look like I am having a stroke?

"I think we've probably got enough pics, eh June?"

"About as many as I can deal with, I'd say," she said, scrolling through her camera reel.

"Great, I'm off to get the Bat Brew out of that bin to calm my nerves." I wasn't entirely sure if I was joking or not. If I wanted Bat Brew from a bin, I should have Bat Brew from a bin, I reasoned. For instance, that tramp we had passed on the way in seemed very happy whiling away his afternoon with Bat Brew on a bench. All these photos, preparation and coordination had just been to please others anyway, I internally grumbled.

The tramp promptly vomited his Bat Brew into the bin Dean had dumped his own drink in and I thought better of my rage fantasy. I settled with silently seething on a bench a safe distance away.

"I come in peace - see, I've put out my sparkler," said Dean, cautiously approaching the bench.

"They're scary, ok?!"

"Did you watch that anti-firework ad when you were a kid?" he asked, taking a seat beside me.

"Yes, and it was very frightening to an over-sensitive child like me!" I couldn't watch The English Patient until I was 26. Even then, it took two bottles of wine and June's promise that she would cover my eyes at the most graphic bits, so severe was my mental scarring after that advert.

"Do you want to know something?"

"What?" I hoped it did not involve the temperature at which your face melts. This was featured in the commercial and had taken me years to forget.

"Do you remember the wee boy whose-"

"Face got melted?"

"Yes! Does he look familiar," Dean turned to show his profile. "Well - before he got burned."

"That was you?!"

"My first acting job! And I must have been convincing if you are still scared 20 years on!" He said with a laugh, but I knew he was mentally adding that to his catalogue of reviews.

I moved around to get a good look at his face. It was handsome, in that sort of 'man in the street who doesn't disgust you' kind of way, I thought, but then I had a traumatic flashback to the ad. "Your face didn't actually melt?!"

"No. It felt like it was melting underneath all those prosthetics though. I haven't told anyone about that for years. All the kids in my class made fun of me for that until, well, I think it was when I became a Goth. That seemed to be even more embarrassing than being 'Burns Boy'."

I tried to stop my impotent pout turning into the trace of a smile.

"Look, life is embarrassing," I relented. "June tried to do a good thing but I'm just not feeling it. Why can't we just be ourselves and not Burns Boy and Anxiety Girl? I don't care what my friends think of me at the end of the day. In fact, are they even really my friends? I haven't seen most of them in at least three years. Don't get me wrong, I still want you to come, but why should we be trying to impress them?"

"You're right," nodded Dean. "The last time I saw my mates from drama school was graduation and I'm still too scared to reply to their Facebook messages asking what I am up to these days."

"I think working in a wine shop with unlimited sampling opportunities is living the dream, to be honest."

"Is it my dream, or is it someone else's? I do wonder, sometimes." Dean looked pathetically rueful.

"Well, we can live the ultimate millennial dream and give a big fuck you to them all."

"See you at the Mini Bar to formulate our cunning plan?" Dean brightened with a smile.

I smiled back, already looking forward to my next visit.

Chapter 13

A week later, I walked into the shop at the same time as usual, a bit like a life-size Bavarian clock that has little villagers pop out of it. There was someone waiting at the Mini Bar, but it wasn't Dean.

Another man was covertly pouring himself a glass of Malbec below a giant sign that read 'Help yourself!' He gave a start when he heard me crack open the screw top of a bottle of white. The Malbec was placed back down on the counter like he had been rumbled shoplifting.

"This is great, isn't it?" His words were mumbled into his glass as he looked at the ceiling, but he was addressing me.

"Erm, it is, isn't it? Free wine!" I raised my glass to him.

"Do you come here often?" My heart plummeted to the bottom of my glass, I hoped he wasn't going to try it on. I had to be semi-social all week and didn't have the energy to humour his advances.

"Oh! I'm sorry, that came across as quite creepy, didn't it!" He clasped his glass closer like a teddy bear. "It's just, I discovered the counter about a month ago and think it's fantastic."

Quite how one discovers something that is advertised in neon writing directly above where it is located, I don't know, but he seemed so happy in a mousey, skittish sort of way that I didn't want to burst his bubble.

"Yeah, it's a good way to try something new," I said with a polite sip. My eyes scanned about, when would Dean save me from the Christopher Columbus of wines?

Mr Columbus snuffled like a little woodland creature as his eyes darted about the red wine selection. "I've only tried the Malbec - it's my favourite. But I wonder what the Chianti is like? And the Merlot? Oh-oh and the Zinfandel!"

"Well, there's only one way to find out."

"You think...I should try them all?!"

"It's what I'd do."

"What one should I start with?" After he said this, I poured myself a Pinot Grigio to ease the process.

"I'm not a red wine expert, I wonder if Dean is about? He usually has good recommendations."

"Oh, yes, Dean is great, isn't he?" Mr Columbus giggled and I could tell that there had never been any danger of him coming onto me, but perhaps Dean needed to watch out. "He gave me a free bottle of Cabernet Sauvignon for joining the mailing list."

"The cheek! The only thing I got was marketing emails!"

"I said to him," Mr C struck a defiant, if slightly drunk pose, "why should I give you my details," a flirtatious hair flick followed. I started to wonder if Dean was hiding from him.

The drama took an intriguing turn: "If I create an account, you'll just use it to find out how much I drink! I don't want anyone knowing that!"

I tried to hide my puzzlement - surely Dean was aware of how much he drank since he sold him all his booze? "It's a wine shop - not the NHS. I don't think they care, or if they do, it's only about getting you to buy more."

"You're so wise," he sighed in between sniffs of a glass of Zinfandel. "I wish I could use this as a fragrance, except it might make look like an even bigger lush than I am!"

Another flick of the hair followed. "So, I worked my charms upon him!" I tried to channel Dean's actor spirit to look convinced, "And he said, "Look, mate" - that's what he calls me, you know, "if I comp this bottle of Cab Sauv, will you give me your email?"

"Not a bad deal!"

"I know he was just after my email, deep down!" the man tittered. "This is very good Zinfandel, isn't it?"

"It must be," I muttered into my glass.

"I think I'll get a bottle. Dean's not here tonight though, so, alas, I may have to pay!"

It seemed like I was the one who was paying for this conversation in Dean's absence. Columbus went to the till and subjected the poor temp to himself for a few minutes while I pretended to study a bottle of wine I had seen many times before. The shop was quiet though and I could tell by the projected huffs of the young shop assistant that they had somewhere better to be, even if I didn't.

I dutifully took the bottle over to the till where it was rung through without so much as a smile. I could feel middle age creeping upon me as I imagined the strongly worded letter I would write to her manager, but then I realised that presumably her manager was Nigel and writing a letter to him seemed weird, like writing a formal letter of complaint to a friend because their toddler stuck their tongue out at you. This thought process had obviously taken too long - the clerk was now staring at me as if I was a clock counting down the last minutes of a life sentence. I decided to put her out of her misery and make for the door.

An hour later I found myself looking at the same bottle I had used as a prop in the shop. This time I was gazing at it as if it was a crystal ball, peering into its depths to see if it would tell me why Dean hadn't been there that night when we had so much to plan. I even gave it a hopeful shake, Magic 8 Ball style. For a moment, I thought it must have done something as my phone lit up, but it was just a group chat I thought I had muted. Having no interest in the teething problems of the child of a vague acquaintance, I swiped the notification away and sunk down into the sofa.

The only company I wanted that night was Riesling des Herr Kolb, a trusty favourite that never disappointed, unlike Dean. It might have failed to give me the answers I was looking for, but I knew I could rely on it for an evening's entertainment, coupled with some trashy TV. I liked to imagine Herr Kolb as a mischievous old man in lederhosen, with twinkling eyes and twitching moustache. Someone who was never short of a joke or two or a laugh that was infectious in and of itself. I'd smile for the first few seconds of this reverie before it turned to a nightmare - imagine having to spend the evening with a relentlessly jovial ageing German who laughed at his own jokes and had God knows what in his moustache that apparently moved by itself.

In fact, I would probably need a bottle of his Riesling just to cope with him. Perhaps that is why he first invented it, so people would tolerate all the lederhosen and laughing. I was distracted by a different laughter now, one drifting in from the street below. I shuffled to the window to see my next-door neighbours gathered round the light of their cigarettes. In the conversation bubbling up, I could pick out the words 'Wes Anderson', 'brewery' and 'Berlin'. I shuddered a little, at the cold or the hipster conversation, I wasn't sure, and shut my window to create a hermetic, or should that be hermitic, seal.

I turned on the TV and Roman Holiday was on. Runaway princess Audrey Hepburn was being pulled out of a river by hunky journalist Gregory Peck after a wild boat party. It was a far cry from the start of the film, which I knew well; Audrey was a bored royal stuck in a dull routine of stale state visits, yearning for a little adventure. Spoiler alert - the happiness was destined not to last, so bound was each to their different life paths. It did seem fun though, taking a break from reality and letting loose like that.

Here I was too, about to go on a crazy trip with a handsome (almost) stranger and break out of the airtight seal I had closed up a long time ago. It might have been a push to call me his Audrey Hepburn though, I think I weigh about the same as two Audrey Hepburns and I have never done anything darling or quaint in my life - and I could never get away with a pixie cut. Dean was a bit Gregory Peck-ish too, though I'd never tell him; it would go straight to his wannabe thespian head.

I had no time to dwell on the implications of all this as Dean's face popped up on my phone.

Dean:

Sorry I missed you tonight

Began the communiqué, followed by dots moving like a worm across the screen, the modern of a montage of pensive writing scenes in an old-fashioned film. I felt that hit we all feel when a message pops onto our phone, like the first sip of wine after a hard day.

I got stuck on a delivery. Spent last 45 mins in a traffic jam.

A vomiting face emoji soon followed.

I was a little disappointed by the brevity of the reply, given the number of dots.

Sam:
It's ok, the shop assistant and I made plans to run away to my reunion together.

Dean:
Oh God, please do. Anything to get rid of her. She does nothing and is so rude.

I laughed a little at the message and plotted my reply whilst swirling my glass. I didn't have time to formulate a response though -

If it falls through with Moany McMoan Face, I'm still up for the job.

It seemed genuine, or as genuine as little letters on a screen can ever appear.

Sam:
I won't demote you just yet. This Riesling has got me in a benevolent mood.

Dean:
Would the I'm Sorry Rosé not be more appropriate?

Sam:
The only thing that wine is appropriate for is setting fire to your enemies!

Dean:
Which Riesling did you go for?

Sam:
Herr Kolb.

Dean:
One of your favourites!

I settled on the sofa with Herr Kolb and smiled as another message popped up on my phone from Dean.

Chapter 14

'Massage & Marriage' was the title of the book June handed to me.

"It's for my coursework. I'm doing one of those online therapy qualifications. I thought marriage counselling would complement massage nicely," she said, with a sweeping gesture around her shop.

I shifted uncomfortably on the sofa, even if I had to marvel at June's entrepreneurial spirit and thirst for knowledge. I was already feeling like I was in a therapist's office. The waiting room's leather sofa squeaked under my sweaty palms and June was peering at me over her glasses.

She had been very concerned about how prepared Dean and I were for the weekend away. I had told her time and time again that we were just going to treat it as a laugh, but it did not raise a smile from her.

"You could be my first clients, if you like!" she said, but I knew it was happening, whether we liked it or not.

"Clients? But I'm not even married."

"No, but you have a big weekend coming up and I think you and Dean should prepare. Even if you are just going to wind people up, it has to look genuine." There was no escape.

"I won't even charge you!" she chirped, but I felt like I would be paying for it somehow.

I left her parlour that night and headed straight to the wine shop to tell Dean. It was better to get it over and done with. I had a feeling it would be less like ripping off a plaster and more like being subjected to a bikini wax by the inexperienced Saturday girl, though.

"Sounds like fun," was his response to the idea.

I was surprised. I was expecting a full-on toddler tantrum at this request.

"Really? I think that is the first time couple's counselling has ever been described as 'fun'."

"I'll think of it as research for my character. Plus, we're not really a couple, so it kind of takes the pressure off a bit. It's not like when my parents went."

"Your parents went to couple's therapy?" I stared accusingly at the glass Dean had poured me, which had clearly made me ask this personal question.

Dean looked deeply into an empty wine box. "Yeah, but they did anything and everything that was featured in the Daily Mail's Sunday supplements in the '90s. They even installed a stairlift when both of them still had working legs," he said brightly, glancing at me at the end as my cue to laugh. I obliged, but it sounded a little canned. I really did try though - I even attempted a smile.

Dean realised he needed to coach me a little more.

"Oh, don't get all early-Ingrid Bergman on me with those glassy eyes and quivering lips! You're not Scandinavian enough, you just look like a confused old person at a bus stop."

"You say we aren't a couple, but you talk as if we have been married for 50 years!"

"Look, some personal info slipped out which you didn't need to know and you don't need to feel sorry for me because I had unhappy parents. It won't be part of the 'weekend package'. I won't start crying and asking why mummy doesn't love me at 4am."

"I mean, you can if you want," I said, catching the pace of the scene. "I think it would really freak out Harriet. Totally worth it." Dean smirked as he sliced open another box. "And it really doesn't bother me if your parents weren't happy. In fact, it would have bothered me if they were. I don't know about you, but it freaks me out when I see happy people. I don't trust them - it must be an act. They probably murder toddlers on the weekend or wear other people's skins in underground sex clubs and it is all part of their cover story. To think you were brought up by two such maniacs would just be too much for me to bear."

"Are you saying that I am not a good enough actor to be a psycho?" Dean clasped his pricing gun to his chest.

"Don't worry, you're certainly self-obsessed enough to be a good actor," I said and sipped the last of my glass. I held it in my hand for a few seconds but the prop began to feel awkward.

"I could get you another one, if you like? There's a Riesling from East Germany called Working Man's Wine that I think you would appreciate."

"Why don't you bring it around tonight? I was going to watch Clerks, it would go well with it."

"Clerks! I haven't watched that in years, though I have been living it."

"Two slackers hanging about a shop and putting the world to rights, I wonder why?" I said, just about keeping a straight face.

A couple of hours later Dean turned up at my door again. This time he was carrying a bottle of wine stylishly named Ink, and its contents looked as if an octopus had been scared to death to make the elixir. It certainly looked potent, but definitely more appealing than the I'm Sorry Rosé.

Normal people probably have genuine other halves turn up with flowers or chocolates, I mused, but the prospect of a night of movies, wine and bitching about customer service could be as intoxicating as romance for me.

"That looks interesting," I said as Dean walked in. "Yes, you're welcome to some, although I know you got a white tonight."

"I think I'll stick to it," I replied as I fired up the laptop.

"More for me," said Dean as he began to take the foil off from around the lip of the wine bottle.

My laptop screen turned from its usual technicolour to the drab black and white of Clerks.

We sank into the black and white world with a sigh, leaving our bland existences behind. I felt myself sink into the sofa and saw Dean's grip on his glass relax a little as Dante fell out of his bedroom cupboard and heralded the beginning of the film.

His eyes wandered from the screen. "You've got a nice flat here, you know," he waved his glass vaguely at the room.

"You can stop being nice to me now, you're off the clock," I said, aware Dante and Randal were glaring at another useless customer on the screen.

"You're not like those people," I let myself have an extra large glug of wine - I clearly deserved it if I had surpassed the mere 'customer' category. "I mean it, it's a very nice place. I like all the folk art," he saluted the tapestries and clay skulls that littered my living room with his glass. "Mexican, is it?"

"Mostly. I've been obsessed with Frida Kahlo since I was nine and read about her at my Gran's in a Daily Mail supplement, of all things."

Dean nodded and contemplated the room and his glass.

"I used to drink to drown my sorrows, but the damn things learnt how to swim."

"Eh?" said Dean. Clerks was now merely background noise.

"It's a Frida Kahlo quote. Can you not see it spelt out on that wall over there? Like those inspirational quotes normal people have - Live, Laugh, Love, that sort of thing?"

"It would be in keeping with the theme and your...devotion to wine," Dean sniggered and his glass jiggled in time.

"Laugh all you like, I've seen you in action too."

"What do you mean?" The glass came to a standstill.

"Oh, well, I suppose I just have to sample that wine with you," I threw a pantomime hand to my brow.

"Yeah, yeah, yeah," scoffed Dean. "I wonder what it would be like if Dante and Randal had worked in a wine shop," he swirled his glass contemplatively, holding it to the light as if he would find the answer illuminated there.

"Probably like your life now, as you said."

"Nah, I mean it might have made them chill out a bit. The customers too. For instance, the guy who has a breakdown and starts smashing eggs into the fridge, perhaps if he had been offered a nice glass of Malbec, this could have all been avoided. I know I've seen a few people at the Mini Bar who looked just about ready to smash eggs."

We might not have been paying full attention to the film, but it was easy enough to follow. It starts with a hapless convenience store clerk arriving at work to find the shutters of his shop sealed shut by chewing gum. His day goes downhill from there as he faces a parade of gormless customers and irritating exes. It's really funny but I could tell Dean wasn't looking directly at the screen. Instead, he would periodically check his phone - I was able to see memes about politicians and a compilation video of dogs riding motorcycles. Eventually, his attention even slid even from that and he just stared down into the depths of his glass.

"Not enjoying the film?"

"Oh, I'm enjoying the film, it's my life I'm not so sure about."

Did I need to hide any sharp objects? I wondered.

Dean could see my concern and laughed. "No, not like that. I just feel sometimes that... I don't know, I shouldn't be living this film, I should be in it. It's funny until you realize it is your life, pretty much."

Dean meditated on the topic for a few moments. "This sounds stupid, but I'm going to tell you - maybe it's the wine. But sometimes I am putting a box of wine away and I'll have this sort of out of body experience. It's almost like I can see myself from above. I go all cold and my heart starts racing. All I can keep thinking is, "Is this it?" Then it's almost like the me who is hovering above real me is shouting "Drop that box right now and run to the nearest audition! It doesn't matter if it's to play 5-year-old female twins, just do it to feel alive!"

Dean looked at me warily.

"Oh," I said casually. "That's just your garden variety existential crisis."

Dean almost looked disappointed. "What do you mean 'just'?"

“I have them all the time. I’m usually sitting at my desk though.” I put down my glass and leaned closer, tapping away at imaginary keys to set the scene. “I’ll be working on a spreadsheet or something equally meaningless. Then I feel a cold shiver run down my back,” I said with a jiggle. “Then I think, just write something, anything else other than this corporate drivel no one actually reads anyway. Write a death threat to your boss with cut-out letters from the newspaper - commit suicide by cop - so you can stop being so scared and just live the life of a penniless author and write about what really makes you happy!”

We both grinned at our sad tales. “I’m glad it’s not just me,” said Dean. Unburdened, he sat back and began to enjoy the film again.

The film finished and so did our bottles of wine. The credits began to roll, and I slid down the sofa a little, promising myself I would crawl off to bed soon. I looked over at Dean, but he was already asleep, and I could feel my eyes gluing themselves shut.

Chapter 15

A few hours later I woke up to a charming hour of the day that I rarely see. The birds were chirping and the sun was lighting up the pond in the garden. A very determined person was even jogging vigorously in the sunshine. I call it 'Airport Hour', a time the average person who is not heavily medicated or insane never sees unless they have to catch the first budget airline flight out of there. Dean was now sloping over the edge of the sofa like a tree after a hurricane, but looked peaceful in a way. It seemed a shame to wake him up, so I tiptoed through the glasses and wine bottles to my room and went back to sleep.

Another few hours went by and I dreamt of being woken up early and forced to participate in a 5am marathon with a bunch of terrifyingly perky joggers. I finally awoke for real with a start in a sweat that could have only be rivalled by actually running a marathon.

When I finally got my breath back and managed to dab enough moisture off my face that I didn't look totally disgusting, I went through to wake Dean up. I found him in the same position I had left him in three hours beforehand. I poked him with an empty wine bottle and his eyes sprang open, confused at finding the world upside down in an unfamiliar apartment.

"Time for couple's therapy!" I chirped. Now it was his turn to have a nightmare.

He slid off the sofa into a pile on the floor, rubbed his eyes and began to morph from decrepit tree into normal human.

June had told us to meet her for brunch at Butch's Bakery, a little patisserie in Beath run by a hulking ex-Death Metal rocker who retired to make pastries after he went to rehab for snorting so much cocaine he tried to swim to a business meeting with Lordi in Finland. Now he sculpted delicate croissants with his hands instead of bashing out anthems on his bass. June raved about his food and usually stopped in once or twice a week to load up on treats, so it was the first place she suggested for our brunch meeting. As a regular, he had let her reserve one of the nooks at the back of the shop for us.

Butch himself brought our coffees and pastries to the table. He was wearing an apron and a flour-covered black t-shirt with a giant red devil with snakes coming out its eyeballs on it. In one massive hand, be balanced a tray of dainty espressos, and, in the other, a tray of sugar-dusted pastries in ornate shapes like little swans and bow ties. He was accompanied by a tangled aroma both powerfully sweet and bitter.

"Your order, Madame," he said to June, laying down his offerings on the table.

"These look delicious as ever, Butch!" said June, helping herself to more than her fair share of his creations.

"Anything for my favourite customer," he replied, a girlish blush appearing on his cheeks.

"Oh Butch, you old charmer, you!" said June, giving him a playful slap on the arm. "I bet you say that to all the girls."

Butch, did, in fact, say it to all the girls. One time I had a particularly bad week at work and stress-ate a box of doughnuts a day from his bakery, and he claimed I was his favourite customer. Likewise, I had heard him trot out the line with multiple girls getting their morning coffee in Beath on their commute. To give him the benefit of the doubt, he had consumed so many drugs in his life that his short-term memory was probably completely shot.

"Only to you!" he told June, before noticing a queue of young women building up at the till. "Oh, it's getting busy, I better get back to work!" he said, nimbly slipping through the network of cutesy vintage tables, despite his huge frame. Before facing his next batch of customers, he blew June a kiss.

"That was almost as sickeningly sweet as these pastries," I said, the swan I had just picked up sticking to my fingers with a fine film of sugar.

"Oh, come on, Sam! Are you telling me you have never flirted with Dean for a cheeky discount?" June said, taking a pointed sip from her espresso.

"No!" I said, a little too loudly for the quiet hubbub of the cafe. Some bored people in the queue craned their necks to see what was going on. I didn't want Dean to get the wrong idea, but he only smiled a little and went back to buttering his pastry. "Don't be such a wind-up merchant, June," I said, giving a huffy shrug.

"Defensive," observed June, producing a notebook and starting to scribble.

"Give me strength," mumbled Dean.

"Do you want to go in my notebook too?" asked June.

"No...

"Good," said June as she produced an egg timer from her bag, turned it over and began her session. "So, the purpose of today is to look at some common challenges couples face and the tools we can use to overcome them," she read from her coursework book, a hefty thing she was now lugging onto the rickety table.

"Tell me, Dr June, is this a challenge you have come across often in your practice?" enquired Dean in his most earnest voice.

"What challenge is that?" June asked thoughtfully.

"That the couple is not actually a couple," Dean said with self-satisfaction; the sabre of his wit had pierced June, he was sure of it.

June did her best patronising smile/laugh combo that struck harder than any sword. Dean's gaze shrunk back to his now empty coffee cup. "Dean actually makes a good point," June conceded, and his eyes sprung up from the depths of his cup. "In a bit of a ham-fisted, patriarchal way," she continued, her teeth glinting like daggers in her tight smile.

"People are individuals first, not couples; sometimes our hopes and dreams involve other people, other times not so much. If the two of you are going to have a working partnership, then you'll need to understand each other on that personal level." Dean had retreated and nodded obediently.

"The two of you know each other quite well, as you are today, but have you ever talked about your childhood?"

"Well -" I began.

"More classic therapy chat June, I was expecting something better from you," Dean said, sitting back and folding his arms, waiting to see how his challenge would be received.

"Dean," June said firmly, her patience was wearing thin. I, meanwhile, had never seen this side to his personality before and June knew it, taking a break from her attack to shoot me a damning look. "As much as I am enjoying the verbal sparring, Sam hasn't said a word yet. I think we should let her go first, don't you?"

Dean flicked a switch and smiled graciously, beckoning me to proceed.

I hesitantly pulled my stool closer to the table, the scraping noise it made on the floor almost as awkward as I felt. "Erm...what is it you would like to know?" was my glittering contribution to the conversation.

"Tell me about your first day at school. I always think you can tell a lot about someone from their first day at school," June said with her pen poised in her hand.

"My first day at school? That's an interesting question." 'That's an interesting question' was a code I had often used in interviews for 'I'm searching for the answer that will make me look the most normal', but June's eyes said 'you can't fool me'.

I surrendered and began to truly search my memory. "I suppose I remember watching everyone else. That probably sounds stupid," I said.

"What do you mean?" Dean and June asked in unison, although her tone was inquisitive and his was more confused. "And no Sam, it doesn't sound stupid," reassured June.

"I remember going into the classroom and just...watching everyone else. All the conventionally pretty girls gravitated to each other and declared they were best friends, even though they had met about five minutes beforehand. It seemed so shallow, it had taken me a good few months to build up my 'best friend' status, which might have been with a teddy bear I had at home, but nonetheless, the whole thing put me off them. The teacher was twisting her hair and giggling at everything my dad did while my mum rolled her eyes. A boy was crying because his Mum was leaving, and even peed on the carpet in protest.

There was a stain there for the rest of primary school. I think the same guy was on Love Island a couple of years ago, actually. I could have made good money out of that story - maybe I still can, thanks for the regression June."

"And that's how you remember everything?" June made a few more scribbles.

"Yeah, it is," I replied cautiously, waiting for a man with a butterfly net to burst out from somewhere.

"Interesting, very interesting," said June. I have sworn she affected a Freudian Austrian twang to her voice.

Dean nodded in agreement. I was clearly one Rorschach test away from One Flew Over the Cuckoo's Nest.

"And what about you, Dean?"

He leaned forward eagerly. "Imagine this - I get out of bed at 5am to shower and dress. It takes me 2 hours to do my hair just right and pick *the* pair of socks. You know how important they can be."

June and I looked at each other - we had finally found the real crazy one in the room.

"Fine - socks matter, okay? I spend an hour rehearsing my introductory speech, "Hi, I'm Dean, do you want to play with the Lego?" It pays off - everyone does want to play with Lego. The rest is history."

I sat back a little to let Dean bask in his limelight. I also wanted to shrink away; surely there was more to him than a lucky Lego set?

"What about when everyone has played with the Lego, Dean, what happens then?" June asked, waiting for the next twist in the tale.

"There is Twister, there is Hungry Hippos, there is Buckaroo..." Dean laughed awkwardly. And then there is yourself, I thought, picturing behind the wine counter, chatting away with the customer of the week.

June scribbled something down and looked at me. Her methods may have been unorthodox, but she understood human nature well enough to know what I was thinking.

"Some interesting perspectives here. The audience and the actor, some may say."

"Excuse me?" Dean blustered.

"Oh, our time is up!" said June. She put her props back in her bag. "I've got an appointment at 12 back at the shop." June grabbed another pastry from the table and hurried off.

Dean shook his head as she left the shop. "She is a strange one. Well, I suppose, don't they say counselling and psychotherapy attract messed up people?"

"Physician, heal thyself," I said, meaning Dean really wasn't one to talk about being a bit dysfunctional.

"Exactly!" he said, thinking I was talking about June.

I gave a resigned sigh and asked, "Shall we go then?"

"Sure, let's head down the road together. My shift starts at 12.30, anyway."

"Oh, OK," I said, rather hoping I could have just made my excuses and headed home by myself.

As we walked down the street, I searched my mind for something nice and normal to talk about, but my brain kept looping round to Dean's little outburst. Was this what he was like in the absence of an hourly wage and free wine? I didn't know if I could afford a whole weekend of him being pleasant if that was the case.

"Are you coming in?" he asked. It was only then it dawned on me that we had already walked all the way to the wine shop.

"Oh, it's OK, I need to pack for the weekend," I mustered.

"Oh. OK. I suppose I'll see you later, then," Dean said.

"Yes!" I said brightly, trying to hide my fear that June and Dean would get into another passive aggressive tête-à-tête. My fear that some slightly strangled fear had slipped out was confirmed when Dean stretched out a reassuring hand to stop me leaving.

"I'm sorry."

“For what?” I asked as if the whole incident had just been wiped from my mind.

“I don’t think I presented the best version of myself in there. I really thought I could not get caught up in my own head and just have fun. Sometimes I just prefer pretending, it’s a lot easier than having to deal with the real ugly stuff.”

“That’s true, but the real ugly stuff is what makes us interesting.”

“Really? I thought it was Lego,” he teased.

“Why Lego?” I asked as we drifted towards the wine shop door.

“Well, it was *the* thing for 5-year-old boys in 1994…”

Chapter 16

"Get in!" said June with a hoot of her horn.

She had arranged to meet Dean and me at the end of Princes Street, the main shopping street in the city. It made the most sense because it was equi-distant from all our homes and would save time for June.

We quickly bundled ourselves into the car and I was glad to watch the parade of tartan-tat and high street chains disappear as June followed a sign for the Forth Road Bridge, the main route north. It wasn't that it was an ugly street or anything. In fact, its huge leafy green public gardens and regal shop fronts often graced the postcards sold on its own pavements. It just never seemed to really change in all the years I had lived here, a sort of living museum to a grand Edinburgh that didn't exist anymore. And right then, I needed a change; my heart fluttered as I stepped into June's car and I realised I was actually a little excited about our scheme for the weekend.

As June's car left the city, I began to feel the years fall off. It was a road I had taken countless times on my way to and from university, and I felt more like I was returning for a new semester than making a cameo appearance in the town's social calendar. The city centre gave way to the suburbs, which led to the Forth and its collection of bridges to Fife. The car cruised on to the newest one, with huge futuristic rods spiralling up into the sky. Next to it were more monuments to the area's past, the historical rail bridge, red and austere, and the older bridge for vehicles that was now living out retirement in the shadow of its younger cousin. June drove steadily, her eyes straight ahead, as I peered down into the white foam on the sea far below. Suddenly a wave of uncertainty hit me: was I crazy to think we could pull it off this weekend?

I half-hoped for some divine intervention. There was still time for the bridge to have a freak collapse and for us to plunge to our deaths. It would probably still be a better way to go than dying of humiliation, which I was becoming increasingly certain was going to happen that weekend.

Dean and June seemed to have called a truce and were having an animated discussion about which version of A Star is Born was the best. I decided to opt out - I had never really connected with the story of the rising female star and her disintegrating matinee idol lover. In the end of each adaptation he kills himself just as she is reaching her peak - which I had always thought was a bit of an inconsiderate last attempt to hog the limelight.

Dean, however, didn't appear to be in agreement. With a beer in hand, he was telling June "It must be hard to be famous. I mean, it's a cross I'm sure I could bear..."

I went back to the view, which had transformed into rolling hills filled with fields and little villages hugging a calm coast. I had always thought that this was the sort of view young boys wanted to die for in World War I, but I had only ever whizzed through it so quickly that I had never made the same commitment. I was always bound for somewhere else, for St Fillan's, which inspired a sort of loyalty that rivalled a love of one's country in its students. That's why so many couples who met at uni went back there to get married in its medieval priory. With its towering spires, snaking ivy and views across its glittering bay, it looked like somewhere everyone's favourite narcoleptic, Sleeping Beauty, might have married her Prince. In fact, it was actually where the Prince of Silesia had married a Princess of Swaziland after they met as undergraduates at the university. However, if Harriet and Allan's wedding had been anything to go by, it was just as likely to be the wedding venue of Fundraising Officers and Logistics Managers, thanks to the alumni discount package.

I caught June's eyes not on the road but darting back angrily towards Dean.

"We'll just have to agree to disagree. You're never going to convince me Kris Kristofferson is better than Bradley Cooper and I'll never change your mind about Lady Gaga. Let's move on to something less contentious. Sam, what is St Fillan's like? I've never been before."

"Me neither," agreed Dean.

"You really need to see it to believe it. Besides, no one believes me when I tell them about it."

"Give us a try."

"Fine. It's basically a small outpost where the middle classes send their children who are too mentally unstable for Oxbridge. Like those odd Kennedy relations who were banished to nice holiday homes on the Cape...there was a documentary about something like that...Grey Gardens? Anyway, the misfits proceed to gambol around this fairytale town with a castle by the seaside for four years with the rest of their kind, before being released back into the wilds of polite society. Hilarity ensues."

"It can't be as bad as all that," reasoned June.

"You have met me, haven't you?"

"Oh, look at those swans over there!" June said awkwardly, pointing to a few flying overhead.

"The swans swim in the sea in St Fillan's," I said wistfully. "It would seem out of place anywhere else, but they seem happy in the bay."

"I was with you up until that swan stuff," said Dean. "I'll have to see it to believe it."

The conversation sputtered out and June put on one of those regional radio stations. We listened to a bland revolving rota of the latest pop music, with one of us occasionally groaning in disbelief at the awful lyrics or the even worse chat from the DJs. Sometimes a cheesy advert for a local car showroom or a funeral home would interrupt the inanity, and June would mutter darkly about the vices of consumerism.

I was glad when we finally reached the sign on the town's outskirts which read: 'Welcome to St Fillan's. Twinned with Canary Wharf & Biarritz.' If we had to listen to that funeral home jingle one more time, I thought June might have a coronary.

A few minutes' later, June's car arrived in the town centre and she let out a clucking sound.

"You didn't tell me St Fillan's had its own moat!"

Dean craned to see but I didn't bother. The moat had almost become part of the furniture for me – having it pointed out to me was like being told there is a sofa in your living room.

Another permanent fixture at St Fillan's was the bridge over the moat. On it, Professor P was smoking moodily and gazing into the sunset, just as he had done for, legend had it, the last 25 years. With him, he had a sketchbook, which he would occasionally furiously scribble in, like a child tackling a colouring-in book with zeal.

"Oh God, I can't believe that he is still pulling that schtick," I said.

"Who?" asked Dean.

"The guy on the bridge. He is one of the art professors here, he must be hanging about for the reunion. A few staff tag along to these things, part of the tradition. Anyway, he hangs out on the bridge, pretending to draw as part of his moody, misunderstood artist act."

"How do you know that he is pretending to draw?" asked Dean, craning to get a better look.

"He has been drawing the same bloody sunset for 25 years!"

June's car rolled to a halt a few metres behind Professor P, who was now stroking his pointed beard thoughtfully. I imagined that he had to squint his eyes at the start of his tenure, but now a scowl of crow's feet (I believe that is the correct term, although some might say it is a gaggle) had taken up residence around his eyes. With a fake start, he closed his sketchbook and dashed towards the car, waving enthusiastically. I wondered what could have inspired such a reaction as he had ceased to find me attractive since I graduated - as soon as you had letters after your name, he wrote 'RIP' across your case file.

Then, I realised what, or rather who, had caught his attention. June was an exotic beauty and, although outside his usual age bracket, he had been known to make exceptions for women from South East Asia. He regularly took 'fieldwork' trips to the region to study the local arts and crafts. These sponsored trips rarely produced anything of note, apart from, rumour had it, a son in Ho Chi Minh and a bar named after him in Chiang Mai.

"Sam," he purred, holding the door open for me. "I haven't seen you since you interviewed me about my exhibition back in your student days." He leaned in closer. "Who is the fox in the front seat?"

"Professor P! Fancy seeing you here." The sarcasm was dripping. "She is far too good for you, that's what she is!" I hissed between air kisses.

"Where are my manners?!" he exclaimed, and I was tempted to reply that he had probably lost them in a boarding school initiation ritual some time around 1972.

He moved to the front of the car and opened the door with a deep bow and doleful eyes. "I learnt this in the Ambassador's Hotel in Bangkok in '89," he said in my ear as he closed the door.

June looked amused, as if she had somehow got involved in a street magician's trick. "Sawasdee," Professor P said, clasping his hand in prayer and dipping so low it was as if he had spotted his last shred of dignity on the ground.

"You've been to Thailand?" June said, against her better judgement.

"I studied traditional woodcarving with some of the masters there. Fascinating place and such," he turned suddenly to gaze at her, "such beautiful, beautiful people." This 'move' wasn't from Thailand, it was from a Mexican telenovela. June almost didn't react; she had obviously heard how beautiful her people were before.

While Professor P proceeded with his mating ritual that had all the subtlety of a randy rhino, Dean had quietly taken our bags out of the car and was standing awkwardly on the sidelines, awaiting his cue.

"Professor P, this is Dean."

"Dean," Professor P extended his hand in the universal bloke-handshake. Dean sniffed equally blokeishly and returned the gesture.

"Doesn't he get the pretty oriental lady treatment?" I whispered.

Professor P patted me on the shoulder, just hard enough to push me out of the beeline he had made for June.

"What's wrong with him?" Dean asked out of the side of his mouth.

"You know in Indiana Jones, the scene in the university? The one where the girls are starstruck and fluttering their eyelashes at him?"

"Yes?"

"Imagine if Indiana Jones hit middle age. Hard. But nobody told him."

"Oh. He does seem like a bit of a knob."

"In a word, yes."

I had done all I could to protect June from Professor P's clutches and, a little disappointingly, she seemed to be entertaining his stories about the old country. As we wheeled our bags away, I even heard Professor P trot out one of his favourite lines: "I have some excellent daguerreotypes of the tribesmen that I would love to show you." I rolled my eyes just in time to catch the glint in his.

Soon we reached the entrance of what was affectionately known as the 'Scandinavian Prison'. From the outside, the complex had even less character, its cookie-cutter blocks straight destined to win no architectural awards - apart from Most Bland Building in existence. From the inside, it looked like an inoffensive flatpack version of The Shining hotel, endless corridors in beige and cream. In short, like a cushy prison at the centre of a tabloid exposé on taxpayers' money.

During our time at university, we had managed to infuse these bland walls with our share of colour and fun, which usually involved propping them up in the early hours after enough cheap beer to keep an actual Scandinavian prison happy for quite some time. The foyer had the same Ikea-style sofa it had always had, though it had been through quite a few incarnations by this point – more than one regeneration due to Harriet. She was prone to using it as a bed after nights out, so much so a dip matching her spine was firmly imprinted after our First Year. There had been an unfortunate incident in which she had fallen asleep on it covered in fake blood after going as Carrie to a fancy-dress party. The result had been so worrying that the police turned up to investigate.

Luckily, they knew the drill a year later when she managed to spill an entire bottle of red wine on it during a particularly doomed attempt to host a sophisticated wine and cheese night.

Now she sat on the same sofa, erect and prim, hands firmly clasped over the handle of a chunky floral weekend bag. She only took up a mere fraction of the surface area, neatly folded into the left-hand corner. She maintained the domesticity of her kingdom by discretely brushing some loose fibres off the cushion next to her.

"Sam!" she trilled with a regal wave. I took a deep breath as I realised our act had begun. "And this must be Dean."

I put my arm around Dean and felt him tense suddenly before quickly relaxing into his role, scooping me up and chucking me on the sofa.

"There's more of that to come later. And you too, if you're lucky." He turned to Harriet with a wink.

Harriet clutched her hold-all close in the absence of a set of pearls.

"That won't be necessary," she clucked as if she had just been offered double glazing by a cold caller.

Allan shuffled onstage, lugging an even larger bag.

"Hello Sam," he said absentmindedly, "Is there anything else in the car, my darling?"

I struggled not to say 'your balls' and Dean saw my lips twitch. Allan became vaguely aware of Dean's presence and offered him his hand.

"Who needs handshakes when you can have hugs?" Dean declared as Allan was enveloped in a bear hug, probably the most physical intimacy he had had in quite some time.

Harriet's eyes were bulging so hard that I feared they may have shot out her head had I not been lying across her like a human seatbelt.

"Just like old times!" I said, picking myself up off the sofa. "Us splayed out on the couch, Allan awkwardly dealing with physical contact."

"I can't say I remember, it was so long ago," Harriet smiled brightly as she relayed her alibi. "So, Dean, what is it you do? Sam never said."

"I'm an actor," he said proudly.

"Oh," said Harriet, in the same tone one might use if given a fatal diagnosis.

The tension was cut by the arrival of the American contingent. A familiar voice grew louder as the automatic doors opened.

"That's the way it is in Iraq, of course I was kidnapped!"

Nicky Spear hadn't physically changed that much since university, but her tales had certainly got taller. She stood in the lobby, her ginger hair closely cropped, in an oddly tight-fitting pair of combat trousers, high-heeled desert boots and what looked like a flak-jacket from a limited edition Barbie Goes to Baghdad set. Apparently she now had a costume to go with her act.

I shouldn't have expected anything else now that she had been unleashed into the big bad world. First of all, she was from Boston, the town in England, and had never crossed the Atlantic when she arrived at St Fillian's. However, she immediately developed a thick American Bostonian accent when she realised how many kids from the States were on her course. There were tales of the Mayflower and ancestors playing key roles in the Tea Party and just the odd slip into her old accent, which she blamed on weakened vocal cords from her career as a child star opera singer.

I remembered another tale she had spun like a deranged dervish at university. There was a rumour that the Department of Political Strategy was really a front for a spy ring, such were the number of former 'diplomats' and 'advisors to [Insert Dubious Republic]' who now worked there. Naturally, Nicky was excited to tell us she had got a part-time job there which required security clearance, working in the offices of the department heads. It turned out that she in fact had a gig as a cleaner and needed the alarm code so she could clean the offices after hours, but she never gave up talking about her work with a wink.

"Getting kidnapped is boring after a while. I think that was about the fourth or fifth time it happened to me."

"Did they sell you into white slavery?" came a voice from behind her, dripping with licentiousness.

"Again? No, I fought my way out with just bare fists," she said, examining a manicured nail.

"Pity," said her comrade, stepping out of her shadow. Paxton revealed himself, still a compact 5ft to Nicky's larger-than-life stories. Nicky gave him a dirty look, but the thrill of an expanding audience soon took over when she spied us.

"Oh, everyone's by the sofa, just like old times! Hugs!!" Nicky said, throwing open her arms and running towards us.

Paxton shrunk back into her shadow, but I made a beeline for him, dodging Nicky with Dean in tow. This didn't go unnoticed by our itinerant Iraqi, her eyes following Dean as we skirted around her.

"Seven. Hours," said Paxton.

"What?"

"I've had to sit next to the female Walter Mitty for seven hours crossing the Atlantic,"

Paxton tugged at his rumpled collar. "Next time I say that travelling with Nicky will be fine, please send some Russians with nerve gas. In fact, you could ask Nicky to recommend someone, since she apparently knows so many former Soviet spies," Paxton produced a small flask and took a gulp.

Nicky had spent the last few years in the States, though no one was exactly sure why. Paxton had met up with her for a drink a couple of times when he went out to California to visit family and mentioned she claimed to be working on an app, but we took that with a pinch of salt so large it would have given us high blood pressure.

"Is this the 'boyfriend'?" Paxton asked with a nudge.

"Indeed I am," Dean said with over-egged conviction.

"Oh, don't worry about that with Paxton. We can trust him."

"Don't worry, Dean, is it? We all tell our white lies. One time I pretended that I was a stockbroker for six months because Harriet always sounded so disgusted when I said I was trying to gamble away a trust fund to avoid a tax bill."

Dean's eyes darted between the two of us as he tried to work out who was the bigger hot mess.

"Now Paxton, I know I can trust you because you never told anyone that I was with you when you were caught drinking the Principal's 50-year-old Port at that welcome reception. Even though I was hiding behind that gold bust-"

"The one of himself he insisted on being shipped in from the Middle East?" said Paxton, falling into a pit of helpless laughter.

"I forgot about that! Didn't he try to justify it by saying the Sultan would be terribly offended if he hadn't done so, and he didn't want to be responsible for another war in the region?"

"That's my favourite part of the story," said Paxton, gripping my arm as if it was a railing that would stop him slipping further into fits of giggles. "Actually, no, my favourite part was when we published that anonymous review of it. It made taking the blame totally worth it," he said, his laugh becoming a hysterical wheeze. Dean looked concerned, almost on the verge of offering him an inhaler, when he finally spoke again, "The Principal almost had a coronary. In fact, they say he did, but I think that was probably down to the mini fridge of brie and pâté we found in his office."

Dean's eyes flicked between Paxton and me, we were both now cackling like hyenas on meth. "Who even are you people? What is this place? An alternate reality where they never cut off Marie-Antoinette's head?" asked Dean.

"And they all ate cake and lived happily ever after," said Paxton, raising a flask that was in his tweed jacket pocket.

"What's your poison?" Dean asked, who had obviously decided if you can't beat them, join them, and cut himself a slice of aristo gateau.

"Glen Lough '83."

"Good choice," said Dean with a blokey nod.

"You know your way around a drinks cabinet?" Paxton said, offering a tip of an invisible hat.

"Well, I can't say I have much experience with the Principal's Port, but I get by," Dean said with a shrug.

"My good man, don't put yourself down. Working in a wine shop is one of my great dreams. Well, if I actually had to work," said Paxton with a wave, summoning a flunky to take his monogrammed bags. They appeared, as if from thin air, and hurried off with his luggage while he and Dean talked wine. Sensing a budding bromance and not wanting to interrupt, I busied myself with a zip on my rucksack, the same one that I had used to bring my stuff to St Fillian's the first time around.

"Why don't we decamp somewhere a little more private for a tasting? We brought a couple of bottles of very nice wine with us which you may wish to sample," said Dean.

"Excellent! I suppose Sam can come too - if she must" sighed Paxton, digging an elbow in my ribs.

"Yes, yes, very amusing," I said, swinging my bag onto one shoulder. "About as amusing as that time Allan tried stand-up comedy."

"You have cut me to the core," said Paxton, gasping with theatrical relish.

Chapter 17

We made our way over to the town's beach, about 10 minutes' walk from the halls. To get there, we had to cross St Fillan's world-famous polo fields. In a staggering case of cultural appropriation, the town council had claimed that they were the oldest polo fields in the world until about 50 years ago, when it became increasingly hard to deny the whole India origin thing. Nevertheless, they still had a reputation as some of the finest fields in the world for the pukka sport, and they even hosted a flashy celebrity tournament every year, which saw Hollywood types, royals and retired sports stars form teams. Even if you hated the sport, you would still come down to the fields for a little celebrity spotting. Plus, there were always town legends about the stars letting their hair down in students digs or riding their horses through town at 3am. All those memories came flooding back as we marched towards the beach, and I mused if I could maybe persuade June to drive up again later in the year for the competition.

"I can't believe you had a beach at uni," muttered Dean, trying to balance himself and two bottles as he hopped over the last fence before the beach. He sunk into the sand, but, true to form, kept the wine safe.

Dean breathed a sigh of relief and Paxton vaulted over like a champion terrier at Crufts. "The wine is definitely in safe hands!" I called as I ran to catch up with Paxton. A pang of guilt hit and I turned to see Dean struggling through the sand, kicking up waves of it as if he was wearing flippers.

"Paxton!" I yelled. He was now down at the water, kicking up his own waves in the sea. "Let's sit up here."

Dean looked relieved. "Thanks, we didn't have Frolicking on the Beach 101 at my uni either."

Paxton bounded back up to us excitedly and grabbed a bottle.

"What's this?" he panted, holding a bottle of Prosecco to the sunlight.

"It's called the Next Big Thing. For when the situation calls for champagne but all you can afford is prosecco."

"I can't say I've ever been in that position." Paxton's grandfather owned half of Chicago, it was rumoured. "But, as Rick Blaine would say, I'm a Citizen of the World, so I welcome all creeds!"

"I think this could be the start of a beautiful friendship," smiled Dean as he poured our glasses.

"Do you remember when we ran into the sea here on my 21st birthday?" asked Paxton, with a glint in his eye that sparkled as much as the Prosecco.

"How could I forget?" I shivered at the memory. "Paxton's birthday is on 21st January, you see."

Dean laughed agreeably, as Royals do when faced by the festive dances of a strange culture.

"You poor guy. You must be thinking, "This is even more uncomfortable than I thought it was going to be," Paxton said with a belly laugh.

"No, no, no," Dean simpered, but Paxton persisted. "The night is young, Deany boy. We will have you rolling about naked in these cruel but beautiful waves by dawn tomorrow."

Paxton pointed a bottle at Dean ominously. Something shifted in Dean; it might have been his alcohol level as he downed a beer. "Challenge accepted," he declared.

Paxton high-fived him and leapt to his feet. "Let's play a game!" he declared.

"Like what? Polo?" Dean scoffed.

"Ha! Sam, do you remember when we broke into the polo club after midnight, stole their mallets and I rode around on your back smacking the ball about for two hours?"

"My back certainly hasn't," I said. June had actually mentioned she thought I had an old back injury a couple of times.

"Anyway, I didn't mean that sort of game. I meant Never Have I Ever! An absolute classic!" said Paxton, pre-emptively pouring three glasses of Prosecco.

"Oh, come on, Paxton, we're not 18 anymore," I moaned.

"What? You scared Dean here will find out something embarrassing about you?" needled Paxton.

"I'm in!" said Dean eagerly.

"I'll start!" Paxton shouted, not even waiting for my response. "Never have I ever...been barred from the student union for climbing up its scaffolding and doing a pole-dance at the top of it!"

I heaved a resigned sigh and took a swig of the Prosecco. "And that's why I don't drink absinthe anymore," I said, not making eye contact with either of them.

"Maybe you should," said Dean. I looked up, a weird ball of nerves in my chest, curious to see how serious he was, but he was already distracted by Paxton pestering him to take his turn.

"Fine, fine. Never have I ever, er, starred in a play?"

We all took a drink.

"I've starred in a few productions, here and there," Dean informed us with a cool shrug. He looked up expectantly, hoping for Paxton to pull the details out.

"Do you remember when I starred as Lady Macbeth?" Paxton asked me, instead.

"How could I forget? It was quite a bold choice for us to stage Macbeth as a pantomime. Also, I played Banquo's Ghost, don't you remember?"

"How could I forget that? I kept corpsing when you would sneak up on Macbeth and the audience yelled, "He's behind you!"

We both tipped back our glasses of Prosecco and laughed even more, but I noticed Dean looking sadly at his.

"Oh, my turn!" I said, determined to swing the spotlight back onto Dean. "Never have I ever...been hideously burned by fireworks on TV!"

Dean smiled and took a big gulp of his drink.

"What's that all about?" asked Paxton, leaning closer to Dean.

"I was in a government advert about the dangers of fireworks when I was a kid," said Dean, halfheartedly waving off Paxton's attention with his free hand.

The next couple of hours followed on a similar loop, until it began to get chilly. Paxton and Dean had challenged each other to a competition of who could strawpedo beer the fastest. I knew I was going to have to be relatively fresh for the rest of the reunion, so slipped away to get some rest as Paxton challenged Dean to a rematch.

Chapter 18

It was about 11.30pm and Dean had not come back to our room yet, despite all the trouble I had gone to in separating the twin beds from each other, leaving as big a gap as possible as the room dimensions would allow.

A 24-hour news channel was on in the background, I hadn't really been watching, but the periodic world weather report was beginning to grate on me. If I heard it was 32 degrees in Dakar one more time, I wasn't sure if I could be held responsible for my actions. I jabbed the off button on the remote and picked up my phone.

I had also come dangerously close to completing Wikipedia that evening, so I decided to message June instead. She had decided to use the day pass for the spa before the actual reunion, but she was probably lying bored in bed now too, I thought.

I looked around the fading, fraying dorm room.

Sassy Sam:
How was the spa?

Comrade June:
Worth every penny! Having cocktails in the hotel bar.

A few cocktail emojis followed. Indeed she was, June only ever whapped out the emojis after a few drinks.

Sassy Sam:
Can I come over? I'm bored.

Comrade June:
Is Dean not keeping you entertained?

I looked over at the empty twin bed in the corner.

Sassy Sam:
He's out with Paxton.

Comrade June:
Still?! They are going to be so hungover tomorrow.

This was followed by some emojis violently vomiting for clarification.

I noticed that she had dodged the offer of my company, so I tried again.

Sassy Sam:
Shall we join them, then? The Farquhar cocktails are so good they are worth the hangover...

A few minutes passed and my phone buzzed again, a small icon of a photo from June appearing on my home screen. It looked like she was with someone in it. Wondering who, I clicked to make it bigger. Then I groaned.

"Professor P, nooooo!" I said out loud. There he was, cosying up to her, martini in one hand and the other one draped over her shoulder. June looked to be enjoying herself, leaning into his chest, tipping a pitcher of vivid red liquid into her mouth. I knew what it was, it was a special request; the Hammer and Sickle she called it, essentially a Bloody Mary with whatever else took her fancy that evening.

Sassy Sam:
Oh God.

Comrade June:
Come over?

A stream of champagne emojis followed.

Suddenly I felt very tired.

Sassy Sam:

Maybe I shouldn't. The reunion is tomorrow night and I want to be fresh.

I was glad she couldn't see me. I wasn't a good actor like Dean and the excuse would have seemed even more flimsy in person. I decided to change the subject, just in case she tried to cajole me into late-night drinks.

Sassy Sam:

What are you doing with Professor P?! He's such an old hack. You could do so much better.

I added a few lovehearts so it didn't seem quite so confrontational. June could get a bit rabid on everything from politics to personal decisions after a pitcher of Hammer and Sickle.

Comrade June:

We've had a very stimulating discussion about post-Communist religious expression in Central Asia. Plus he's not that bad. The bar is quite dark. That helps.

I put my phone back down. June was perfectly capable of making her own bad decisions. I was also already in my pyjamas and an ill-advised crusade against whatever going on with Professor P would have involved putting on proper trousers again, and it did not rise to that level of crisis.

Pulling the duvet round my shoulders, the phone buzzed again. It was probably June, and I did have a certain morbid curiosity about what would happen with Professor P. I pulled it close, and it was a message from her:

Comrade June:

If you won't come out, get Dean to come back! He could keep you company...

Sassy Sam:

I don't know what you mean.

But maybe I did.

June helpfully illustrated what she was getting at with a row of aubergine emojis.

Comrade June:
There was definitely a moment in the car. And when we were at the coffee shop. And at the photoshoot.

Sassy Sam:
Step away from the Hammer and Sickle.

I put my phone face down on the bedside table and turned away. The moments that June talked about still played in my head when I closed my eyes though, like the rolling news and weather in Dakar, but I wasn't sure if I wanted to turn them off.

On my way to breakfast the next morning, I passed by Paxton's room, figuring they may have had a bromantic sleepover after I left them.

On Paxton's door I found a note – 'Gone Swimming', so I headed to the cliffs, briskly shuffling along the chilly cobbled streets - the sun had appeared not to get its wake-up call.

As I approached, I could see two figures on the Pier Point Cliff. It was one of the many town traditions that every student had to jump off it once before graduating, and it seemed that Paxton was determined to confer some sort of honorary degree on Dean. Two figures were huddled on its edge, one significantly smaller than the other, bouncing like buoys in rough seas, wrapped in hotel towels. Soon the smaller of the two whipped off his towel and plunged into the sea, a pink flash literally streaking into the waves. A holler shot up from the water and along the street towards me. As if I didn't know already that it was Paxton, he proceeded to do some flips in the water like an excited dolphin at an aquarium show.

Meanwhile, Dean was still on dry land and more like a dog being stubbornly dragged to the vets. He edged closer and closer, swaying uneasily on the rough water's edge.

Eventually a gust of wind caught him unawares and he tumbled, towel and all, into the waves below, much to Paxton's delight. Paxton is the sort of guy who always manages to sniff out trouble, but it's better to go along with his plans than swim against the tide, as Dean was finding out.

I climbed down to the rocky water's edge and looked at the two of them, my teeth chattering at the mere sight of the water.

"Dean lost his towel!" called Paxton merrily.

Dean shivered in confirmation.

"It's a shame that the town has such strict anti-nudity laws, isn't it?" I called.

"But we just jumped in the sea naked!" shouted Dean over the sound of the waves - one of which smacked him in the face. He was powerless to defend himself though, as his hands had gone below the water in an ill-fated attempt to cover his modesty.

"There is an old by-law that means you can be naked in the water, just not out of it," explained Paxton as he swam back to dry land.

"I don't think I can spend the rest of my bloody life in here! What am I? A merman?!"

"Looks like you'll have to share this," I said, chucking Paxton's towel to him just before his lower half emerged. Dean's towel drifted pathetically out of the bay in the distance. He reluctantly swam towards the ladder leading out of the water. At first slowly, then with increasing pace as he saw one of the famous swans make a Jaws-like beeline for him. "Told you," I said more to myself than anyone else.

Paxton awaited him at the top and threw his arms (and towel) out flasher-style as Dean reached the top.

"I've heard about this sort of thing at these posh universities. One of those homoerotic hazing rituals," grumbled Dean as he manoeuvred the towel over his shoulders, enveloping both Paxton and himself.

"I'm so glad we are on the same page," said Paxton, pulling the towel tighter around their quivering bodies, much to Dean's alarm. Now they had to face the Walk of Shame (or glory, as Paxton called it) back to the halls through St Fillian's streets. Without anything to cover their modesty, other than the towel. Paxton had insisted that leaving all your clothes in your room was tradition, apparently. It was not.

We made our way through the town and I began to feel that Dean and Paxton were like some curious dog breed as people stared at our little group with a mixture of bemusement and fear. I smiled politely, almost having to stop myself from adding 'they don't bite' as we walked through the main thoroughfare.

That was until the wind picked up, somewhere around the town chapel. We passed an orderly queue of elderly women filing out after a service, and I quickened my pace to avoid the disapproving glares. Paxton and Dean lagged behind, moving as they were as some sort of poor attempt at a human centipede. I heard a collective gasp behind me and turned round to see Dean trying to wrestle the towel back over both of them in a whoosh of wind.

It appeared I had probably missed their most exposed moment, all I really saw was a blur of towel and flesh, which were both the same shade of bright pink.

I felt a claw-like grip on my arm and turned to see one of the ladies of the congregation grinning up at me. "Those are two fine young lads," she winked. "Especially the tall one. Not seen the like since those Polish soldiers were stationed here in 1942." She gave me a wink and shuffled off.

"What had I missed?" I wondered, as Dean gave me a shy smile, wrestling Paxton back into the towel. And exactly how fit were those Polish soldiers, anyway? A girl needs a frame of reference at the very least.

Aside from the public nudity, we remained as low key (as possible, in the circumstances) on our way back to the Halls. Harriet was watching us from the bridge as if we were surly shop assistants and she wanted to speak to our manager. I shrugged my shoulders and Paxton doled out another wink. Dean, finally getting into the spirit of things, even said, "Don't judge our love," and shuffled a little closer to Paxton, which elicited a scream of delight from his travelling companion.

"Don't you want to come in, lover boy?" asked Paxton as he slipped out from underneath the towel and deftly (and somewhat unsettlingly) hid his modesty behind his bedroom door.

"Be careful what you wish for," Dean replied, whisking the towel around himself as if he was Dracula about to stalk off into the night.

Chapter 19

That night was our reunion dinner in the Halls' cafeteria. I saw the menu for the evening was up when we arrived back from the beach, so went over to take a look. I made the sign of the cross as I approached, remembering what passed for cuisine during our student days. Back then, anything with a tomato-base was labelled moussaka and served until the food-poisoning cases became a PR problem. Dessert was usually a forlorn apple just days' away from being mulchy cider. Today, the menu was a lot fancier, it was even printed in a flowing script, instead of the moussaka-speckled scrawl of the cook. I saw that we would be served a selection of finger food, most of which featured a salmon mousse or carpaccio of something. Then there was a buffet of pheasant curry, stuffed peppers and swordfish, followed by an assortment of actual sweets. Paxton's family had obviously made another large donation to the alumni fund. Nostalgia is a weird beast though and I even found myself getting a little misty-eyed about the terrible dinners I had almost lost my lunch over a decade before.

The reverie was interrupted by something that was making my stomach turn in the present day - the reunion meal itself. Although we had an unlikely ally in Paxton, I haven't really enjoyed a big social occasion since I danced on a table to Hit me with your Rhythm Stick at the Graduation Ball. I had found it wasn't really acceptable in polite society beyond this town's walls - but was acceptable with a bottle of wine in your own flat on a Friday night.

Now I had no idea what a lot of my classmates had become. Sure, there were the family albums on Facebook, the Instagram photos of the fancy 'date night' meals they shared with their heavily filtered partners, and the LinkedIn accounts which depicted most of them as leaders of the free world, even if the job title was 'Junior Account Assistant [Temporary]'. But what was going on behind the smoke screen of the internet? Were they all as much of a mess as me? Were some of them actually functioning adults?

"Don't be so nervous," called Dean from the bathroom as I unscrewed a tube of foundation with shaking hands and sent the lid flying underneath his bed.

"How do you know I'm nervous? The door is closed and everything," I said, preparing to fish it out by hiking up my dress so it didn't get caked in God Knows What from the room floor.

"I can hear you rustling back and forth in that dress like a swarm of bees or something."

I gave my dress an extra swish, just to wind him up. It was true though, I was nervous, and the dress was one of the '50s style numbers with a massive skirt and tulle that announced your presence before you even entered a room.

Undeterred, I pulled the dress a bit higher and lowered myself down to the floor. I wasn't really sure why I was bothering to protect it so much, it wasn't a new number, it was the same dress I had worn to the Graduation Ball. It had seen a lot worse that night; the rose petal pattern almost totally hid the vat of Sangria Paxton accidentally tipped on it and most of that had completely come out in the wash. It even survived wading into the sea to fish Harriet out at 3.30am. Okay, so a little of the tulle was ripped but I could pretend that was a stylistic choice. I didn't see why I couldn't trot it out again, I doubted anyone would look at it that closely, anyway. Besides, I liked that it had a vintage style. It reminded me of carefree kids in 1950s movies. You know, the ones who went to diners and had hot fudge Sundaes and didn't let silly little things like the Cold War bother them too much.

I was just about to grab the bottle top, my face perilously close to some old chewing gum, when I heard the bathroom door click open. I turned round to see a pair of jaunty red socks at eye level.

"Is this what they call 'presenting' in the animal kingdom?" said Dean behind me. I suppose it did look like that, my arse in the air and skirts flipped back.

I snapped back up, lid in hand. I turned round fully to see Dean in an attempt at black tie. It would appear the only 'black tie' he had was one of those novelty piano ones that played music when you pushed a button.

I blew some floor fluff out of my eyes. "Even if it was, I wouldn't worry, that tie works as an amazing contraceptive," I said, rustling over to my side of the room.

"Hey, come back here a second," said Dean, laying a protective hand on his tie.

"Urgh, what, I have to make myself look halfway presentable," I said, stomping back across.

Dean beckoned me closer and I stepped forward cautiously. Was he known as the 'Piano Man' serial killer and going to garrotte me for insulting his lovely tie? It did sound like something you would find in the stranger corners of Wikipedia. He stroked the side of my face with the back of his hand, which I thought was strange as I hadn't even put foundation on yet and knew I had a massive spot. I wondered if this was something almost as mortifying being locked in a hotel room with a murderer - was this emotional intimacy? I wasn't sure if I was averse to it necessarily, he didn't look bad in the suit, despite the horrendous tie, he seemed to tolerate my jokes and hadn't run screaming when my butt was thrust skywards.

"Whereas this chewing gum only adds to your loveliness, like a beauty spot," he said, brushing the old chewing gum I had last seen underneath his bed off my face.

"Thanks for that," I said, turning away quickly. "Now we just have to hope someone vomits on that tie tonight to make it more visually appealing."

I walked over to the mirror and squirted some foundation onto my hands and massaged it into my face, trying not to think too much about the rancid chewing gum that had been stuck to it moments earlier.

"Don't worry so much. This is an act we have rehearsed," said Dean, throwing on the last pieces of his costume, a black dinner jacket and sunglasses combo that made him look like a third Blues Brother who maybe did some catalogue modelling on the side. "Plus, you look great in that dress. Paxton will probably hump your leg."

I rubbed the foundation in harder to cover up the redness in my cheeks - this was way too much complimenting for me. The closest thing I had had to praise in a while was June told me I had strangely overdeveloped neck muscles.

"It's not that. OK, maybe it is a bit. But I haven't seen most of these people in years, what are we going to talk about?" I said, busying myself with my toiletry bag.

"I would go straight for Princess Diana and/or Maddie McCann conspiracy theories if I were you. That's my plan, at least," said Dean, "I could even make a tinfoil hat to complement my topics of conversation," he added.

"I do love a good conspiracy theory," I mused. "I'm just not sure I'm in the mood for being judged for 4-5 hours by increasingly drunk members of the country's middle management."

"How do you know they're all middle management?"

"I'm taking an average of what they all brag about being on LinkedIn."

Dean laughed. "You'll get through it somehow. As part of my services this weekend, I am always available for bitching and moaning, madame."

He preened a little in the mirror. "Got to look good for you. That's part of the package too," he said with a tip of his sunglasses and a wink.

I was standing by the standard-issue student digs desk, which had been crammed into the room a whole two feet from my bed. It managed to radiate exam stress from all the students who had been hunched over it. The piece of furniture had been hastily disguised with a tourism brochure ahead of the reunion, which I began to leaf through to stop the flashbacks of a particularly traumatic exam season in 2011. "You know, if you are good at this fake boyfriend thing, you could make quite the business out of it."

"You think?"

"Oh yeah, you could place an advert in one of these magazines. A few years ago I was in Amsterdam and their hotel room brochure thingies are full of ads for ladies and gentlemen who provide 'company'. Obviously, it's a bit different in these circumstances, but there must be loads of people who need someone to play their boyfriend."

"So, you think I'm an escort," his sour expression reflected in the mirror, like a bum note produced by his comedy tie. I couldn't help but snigger a little, even though I sensed his mood had shifted. "It's not funny," he said grimly throttling his tie.

"I'm sorry, it was just a joke." I put the brochure down and backed away slowly.

Dean was committed to his brooding by this point and darkly busied himself with his cufflinks. I didn't think it was possible to fasten your cufflinks with the psychotic stare of Buffalo Bill, but somehow Dean did it.

"We'll discuss this after dinner," sniffed Dean.

"Jesus Christ! I am getting all the worst bits of a gigolo and a husband. I have to take you everywhere, come up with a cover story and deal with passive aggression. We're not even going to bang at the end of it." I felt my voice rise at the end of my rant, as if the last sentence was turning into a question.

Dean sighed heavily in response.

"You know what," I took a deep breath and summoned the coup de grâce every woman knows well: "Fine". The whites of Dean's eyes flared but it was too late for such distress signals. "Let's go," I added, the way I imagined Lady Macbeth might have done had her life devolved into a bad rom com like this; perhaps I could confer with Paxton about it later.

Chapter 20

After our first spat, I held the door open for Dean and he shuffled out as one would towards the gallows.

He walked down the corridor, constantly checking over his shoulder, like I might pounce at any moment. I fixed a smile to my face, which just seemed to unnerve him more.

He gave a start when Harriet and Allan's door opened a few rooms down. I recognised the same expression on Harriet's face as on mine and Allan was even walking with the same doomed shuffle as Dean. Harriet picked up on it too and gave a nod of acknowledgement, followed by a flash of hunger in her eyes as she realised there was gossip to be had. Dean and Allan shared their own nod - that of partners in an execution double bill.

We all waited at the elevator in a stony silence, which was only interrupted by a familiar cackle from within the lift shaft. There was a 'ding' and Paxton appeared.

"Are we ready to party like it's 2009?"

We managed a collective, weak smile in response. "Come on guys! Who died? Our career prospects? We never had any – we studied Arts and Humanities during the recession. Let's eat some avocado toast, load up on overpriced cocktails and do something stupid."

"I've done enough stupid stuff to last a lifetime," I said pointedly.

"There's always room for more," reassured Paxton, pulling out a pair of '2009' comedy glasses. Harriet gave him a glare so hard he could see it through the heavily shaded lenses.

"What? It was our Freshman year and it's a reunion, not a funeral, baby." He emphasised his point with a hip thrust towards Harriet before springing out of the elevator and into the lobby. I momentarily forgot my sulk and leaped forward too. Dean's eyes brightened as he entertained the possibility he had been forgiven by proxy, but they soon dulled when I shot back a scowl. Ironically, our couple act was becoming realistic. We were just high achievers, shooting straight past the honeymoon stage and heading to the most advanced level - warring spouses.

I pranced off after Paxton, the millennial Pied Piper who would no doubt lead us all off the Pier Point before midnight.

I followed Paxton over to a group of vague acquaintances. I nodded randomly as they made some chit-chat, hoping I wasn't agreeing with anything too awful. Dean, not without a sense of duty or at least customer service, came to my side. Virgil Kemp, who used to edit our student newspaper, finally acknowledged my presence after talking to Paxton for a few minutes.

"Sam Chambers! It's been a long time!" he cried.

I would like to think we all grow out of those awkward style stages eventually, but he looked exactly the same as he always had; like he was a child in a dressing up box. He insisted on wearing a trench coat three sizes too big for him and a suit that was so ill-fitting it threatened to capsize his stringy body. A cheap ballpoint pen waggled behind his ear every time he laughed too much at someone's joke – which was often. I had heard he was writing for a small-time history magazine based in Norfolk, something he must have got through his commitment to method acting as a journalist from the 1940s.

"Virgil, our fearless leader in the flesh," I replied. Paxton snorted into his champagne glass. It reminded me that I was really going to need one as a prop for the evening.

Virgil gave a thin-lipped smile. "That's very kind of you," he said pointedly, "but we all know who the true talent was at the Fillan Free Press."

A series of nods rippled round the group. I swiped a glass from a passing waiter. Another followed with a trayful of the salmon appetisers, and I grabbed a fistful. "Who was that?" asked Dean innocently and I glared in return.

"Sam, of course!" The words sounded complimentary, but Virgil had the delighted expression of a torturer readying his special spikes for a long day of disembowelling. More nodding followed.

"She is very talented," said Dean, wrapping an arm around my shoulder and planting a kiss on my head. He smiled as if I was forgiven.

Virgil, a stranger to praise and emotion, looked on quizzically. Regaining his composure, he asked with a sickly little smile, "Is Ray Meehan coming tonight?"

The chatter in the group ceased with a collective gasp. Eyes looked everywhere apart from me. Well, Virgil kept his firmly clamped on my face, but everyone else pretended they suddenly found a stain on the ceiling or alumni portrait incredibly interesting. It dawned on Dean that this was something to do with me. I could feel his eyes slide up towards my face, which suddenly felt very hot and red.

There has been something of a ban on mentioning Ray Meehan around me since we graduated. I take a very Stalinist Purge approach to people who cross me, removing the undesirable element completely from my history. Ray fell into that category, and most people knew not to mention him around me. Of course, Virgil knew, and that's exactly why he did it.

Ray and I met on day one of Freshers Week when we were both signing up for the student newspaper. I overheard him passionately arguing that Friends was better than Cheers, and so began an argument, and a relationship, that lasted almost four years. Virgil capitalised on our debates by posing our contrasting opinion pieces next to each other, our two portraits eyeing each other, ready for battle, on either side of the page. Ray always had the good ideas, but he knew I edited both pieces alongside Virgil, and it was sort of an open secret in the town. He always said he didn't mind - he was more of an ideas man after all. Besides, he said I was the really talented one so it could only make him look good, and sometimes I almost believed him. I am so lucky to have such a supportive boyfriend, I thought at the National Student Journalism Awards, where we were head-to-head for columnist of the year. I won, but here was Ray posing proudly next to me on the stage, a heartwarming smile across his face.

I thought that I was lucky throughout our relationship, until Ray very abruptly reneged on our plans to move in together and pursue our literary careers in the big city. He "had to go home for a bit and take care of some things". Weeks turned into months, which turned into one of the earliest, pioneering cases of ghosting. Then, in what became one of my increasingly aimless trips to a bookshop, I saw a familiar name out of the corner of my eye: 'Ray Meehan'. Doing a double-take, I walked over to the 'New Releases' display case, where I was confronted with hundreds of signed copies of 'Four Hundred in Four Years: The Diaries of a Sex-Mad Student'.

I didn't bring him up with new acquaintances like Dean because they always rushed to buy a copy to get all the dirt. It's really more humane to spare them the horror of reading his hackneyed dialogue and cringe-worthy sex scenes and will also spare him the royalties. The gist is that dear faithful Ray had actually been on a sex odyssey during our relationship but had neglected to let me know. Thankfully, he 'always knew he had a spark of genius and no longer wanted to live in [his] girlfriend's shadow', so had retired to his parents' house post-graduation to write his memoirs. Which, rather irritatingly and humiliatingly, became the talk of the town and an international bestseller. This time I couldn't rise to his challenge and pen a retort - so I promptly slunk into obscurity, never sure I would write again outside the safe bubble of annual reports and social media posts for other people.

"Ray Meehan? Didn't he write that sex book a few years ago?" said the innocent Dean.

Delighted, Virgil pressed on. "Oh, didn't you know? Sam and Ray were an item at uni. She was the..." his voice lowered to a delighted hiss, 'the girlfriend.'

Now everyone started staring very intently at the same spot on the carpet.

"Oh, *that* Ray," laughed Dean. "I totally forgot you had a thing with him. She moves in very artistic circles, you see. I actually stole her away from Michael Fassbender. You were getting tired of always being someone's arm candy, weren't you Sam?"

Various twitterings went round the circle, but they were drowned out by Virgil positively fizzing with rage. I think he was hoping that he would drop his gossip bomb and I would immediately burst into tears or flames or something, giving him ample gossip for the rest of the evening.

"It was very difficult for me," I confirmed. "But to answer your question, I don't know where Ray is. There are only 365 days in the year, and, if you read his book, you'll know that he has a very busy schedule indeed. I imagine whittling the notches in his bedpost alone is a fulltime job."

Laughter spread round the circle like a Mexican wave, but stopped dead at Virgil, who decided to try a different tack.

"Anyway, enough about him. What have you been up to for the last five years?"

Now it felt like the entire group's eyes were turning on me like one of those bright lamps detectives have in the movies. "You were going to write a book, weren't you?" Virgil twisted the knife.

"She's working on it," said Dean with authority. "It's all very hush-hush, of course. Her publisher wants to keep her identity secret to increase the sales," he winked. "You must know what it's like, you're..."

"Part-Time Contributor at Memory Lane Magazine," mumbled Virgil, the group drawing glasses to their lips to hide their smirks. "It's the most popular title among the house-bound over-85s."

"Absolutely fascinating," said Dean, almost convincingly.

"Oh yes, it's really only a matter of time before your memoirs come out Virgil, don't give up hope," I said, clinking my glass with his. Linking arms with Dean, I gave Virgil a little regal wave and glided towards the bar.

"Nice save," I whispered when we were safely out of earshot. He might have been a bit overdramatic about my escort comment, but he was actually pulling this off. "Listen, I'm sorry if I touched a nerve with that stupid comment back in the bedroom," I said, trying to suppress an awkward squirm.

"Forget about it, I already have," said Dean as we leant on the bar. He placed a hand on top of mine and leaned closer. I almost forgot how sticky the bar always was and always would be, but then again, I am trapped in the prison of an over-thinking brain, so wasn't swept up in the moment as much as one might have been. Without the hesitation I felt coursing through my veins, Dean kissed me as if it was something he did every day before leaving the house for work. I wasn't sure how I felt about it, half-happy he didn't consider me totally unkissable, and half-confused about whether this was part of the game we were playing. There was no time for me to fully digest, obsess and worry about the situation though as I could feel the distracting presence of someone looking at me. I turned away from Dean, who was smiling at either a job well done or something else, to find Nicky's eyes boring into us.

"What a cute couple!" Nicky fizzed. "I was just talking to Josh and Hudson. Do you remember them? They were my flatmates in Third Year. They're married now, can you believe it? Maybe you two lovebirds will be the next to walk down the aisle." Where was the waiter, when could he bring me the wine and how much would it take to kill me, I wondered.

"I was almost married in Mauritania, you know," continued Nicky, and I began to make desperate eyes at the barman, trying to blink out 'SOS' in Morse Code. No luck, we were trapped with Nicky, destined to be tortured for more information, mostly by her awful fashion sense; she had chosen a tight leather dress she seemed to have borrowed from the Matrix trilogy and a long velvet cloak. I was prepared to admit the whole charade if she would just wear something less offensive to the eyes.

Undeterred by our silence, Nicky pressed on. "But that was another life," she shrugged. Yes, one you never actually lived, I mused internally. Nicky might have been a fantasist with the sartorial elegance of a Disney villain on hard times, but she wasn't stupid. Her eyes narrowed and moved away from me to focus appreciatively on Dean.

"And who exactly is Tall Dark and Handsome? I don't think we have been properly introduced. I recognise you from somewhere though, have you done any acting?" I managed to just about suppress a gag - who did she learn her pick-up lines from and why weren't they at the bottom of the sea wearing concrete boots?

I could tell Dean had the same thought as he glanced at me and laughed under his breath. A couple of seconds passed though and the flattery was just too much for his inner actor's ego – down to the bottom of the sea he went.

"A little, when I was younger," he smiled bashfully - perhaps I was giving him too much credit for his acting.

"Anything I would have seen you in?"

No, not unless you have a fetish for fire safety videos and student productions of Fiddler on the Roof, I thought.

"It was very low key," he shrugged.

"Do you still do any?" asked Nicky, looking at him like he was in an audition for her next fantasy.

"No, not anymore."

I began to wonder if the pattern of my dress was too similar to the wallpaper and I had become invisible.

"Why not?"

"Life kind of gets in the way," he said ruefully.

"Well, I might have an opportunity for you. I actually have my own little entertainment business that you might be interested in," Nicky said, fumbling in her handbag. "I must have left the cards in my room. I'll go get you one right now."

I raised an eyebrow. "You do that Nicky," I smiled.

"So nice to meet you, I'll be back soon," she said to Dean and tottered off.

Dean smiled dreamily into his pint.

"You know, I really think you might be the most handsome man I've ever met. You are the other half of me, the light of my life, let's get married," I said.

"Eh?" Dean jolted back to reality.

"Well, apparently flattery will get someone everywhere with you, and I could do with another glass of wine, so I thought I should really go for it."

Dean rolled his eyes. "It's nice to get a compliment every now and then. Even if her business is about as real as that 'champagne' they have been passing around," Dean said.

"I know, it's Cava at best, isn't it?" I said, looking at a sad tray of untouched fizz.

"It wouldn't surprise me if it was box wine and soda water," said Dean. "Still, free drink is free drink. I'm interested to see what the food is like, shall we head in?"

He offered me his arm and we joined the crowd heading towards the dining room.

Chapter 21

Plumes of smoke caught my eye and I remembered the Fag Ash Bench with another nostalgic twang. I had never smoked myself, but Paxton had a thing for cigars and I had spent many hours of procrastination loitering out there with him - and Harriet - who insisted that smoking was the most disgusting habit in the world until the tequila came out, then she became a chain smoking fiend.

The warm and fuzzy feelings soon gave way to irritation when I saw June and Professor P on the bench, illuminated by the temperamental flicker of the streetlamp above them. I could also see Nicky coming back waving a card in the air and my heart sank a little further; I knew I couldn't sit through another gross-out episode between her and Dean so left him to his fate. There was still time to save June, I reasoned, but he had dug his own grave after being run over by the Nicky flattery train.

"I'm going to rescue June, have fun with Nicky," I said breezily.

"Don't leave me alone with her," he mouthed as she approached, before snapping on a smile as she reached his side.

It was a place the Professor knew well, often stopping for a fag on his way to lectures. Most of the crew who staffed the bench were actually not in attendance at the reunion. Back in the day, Paxton, Harriet and I would scuttle away as they approached, desperate to avoid Death by Discussing Sartre and How Everything is Beneath You, which I believe is Chapter 1 in the Wannabe Radical Student Handbook. These had been Professor P's compatriots - they were too cool for something as mainstream as a reunion. He would need to drag someone out for company, and June had stumbled into his trap.

"The thing about Sartre was..."

It seemed a pity to interrupt such an assured performance, one he had been refining for 25 years now. If I hadn't seen him discuss the intricacies of French philosophy hundreds of times, I would have thought he was so carelessly cool as he tossed his head back and released a thread of smoke into the air, rather than shuttering through the motions like a rickety fairground ride.

"Hi guys!" I beamed. I could see the Professor glaring at me, even through the smoke that followed him like that cloud follows Eeyore. "June, I didn't know you smoked?"

"Normally I think that tobacco is a capitalist conspiracy to preserve indigenous underclasses across the globe." She took a long drag, "but sometimes I like to let loose," she shrugged. "How is Dean? Living up to his end of the bargain?"

"This sounds like a good story," the Professor stepped out of his smoke cloud.

"It's not," I replied. I knew he couldn't be trusted with the story and knew it was time for me to bow out. June would just have to fend for herself.

"Be careful," I warned her.

"You too," she replied. "But not too careful, ok?" She blew out a steam engine-worthy burst of smoke, obscuring both herself and Professor P. It was probably for the best, I thought as I headed back inside; I wasn't sure my eyes could cope with much more of the slow motion car crash that was my best friend copping off with my crinkly old lecturer.

Chapter 22

The Halls' automatic doors juddered open for me and the first thing I saw was Allan and Dean, who were sipping beers at the bar. Poor Dean, I thought, Allan had likely cornered him to discuss the merits of Toyota's latest hatchback, and just as we were being called in for dinner, too. At least he was at the bar, that would numb some of the pain.

Nicky was long gone. She must have found another poor unsuspecting victim. It dawned on me that Harriet was no longer beside Allan, grimacing like a displeased parrot on a pirate's shoulder. I gave a start when I realised she had fluttered off and settled on mine instead.

"You won't believe what Allan just told me," she said out of a corner of a smile.

I tried to pretend I was suddenly fascinated by an old painting of a dead white man in front us, but it was no use.

"He wants us to...have a threesome."

Now here was some juicy gossip I could actually get engrossed in.

"Allan? Really? I always thought he was more interested in digestive biscuits than sex."

"So did I!" blurted Harriet, drawing a few eyes from the dinner crowd. Longing for obscurity, she grabbed me by the arm and pulled me into the throng.

"Why are you telling me this, anyway?" I asked, as she manhandled me towards the dining room.

"Well, you are a woman of the world, aren't you?" she said, steering me towards our group's table.

"What does that mean?" I asked, already knowing that I would not like the answer.

"You know...you drink wine, not tea, you go on holiday instead of having children, you have brought a 'Thai masseuse' and a randy gentleman caller as your guests, not a husband. You know, you're everything that I'm not."

I took a deep breath and twisted a fancy napkin on the table in my hands, just to keep them busy, lest the temptation to strangle her grew too strong. "I'm sure there was a compliment in there somewhere, but I'm not sure how I can help," I said robotically.

"You must have come across something like this before."

"Do you think us women of the world have trouble keeping men with all our wine, holidays and Asian sex workers?" Someone I recognised from First Year Classics raised an eyebrow in our direction.

"Don't let anyone say that Sam Chambers doesn't know how to have a good time," I winked.

Harriet was thoroughly mortified. "Oh Sam, you're such a joker! It's what I love about you!" she said through a rictus grin, once again dragging me off. I almost felt dizzy. It was like a never-ending ceilidh dance being swung around the floor this much.

"I should have known it would lead to something like this," she muttered furiously. We were now back by the old reception sofa, which she plonked herself down on, like a child on the naughty step.

"You're going to have to fill me in. I may be a 'Woman of the World', registered trademark Harriet Benson, but I am not a mind reader, just a skanky sex-mad lush," I said a little loudly, just to wind her up.

Harriet narrowed her eyes, but there was no hiding their expression - they said 'shut up' in 100 languages.

"Urgh, I shouldn't be angry at you," she relented. "It's all WebMama's fault."

I sat down too and began to wrack my brains. Why was it WebMama's fault? It was an online forum for yummy mummies who debated whether gender reveal parties were cute or transphobic, not something I could see Allan getting mixed up in that easily.

"How has WebMama's driven Allan to abandon monogamy?" I felt like I was back in a Maths class at school and hadn't paid attention to how the equation should work. Harriet looked at me with her best 'disappointed schoolmarm' expression.

"Keep up Sam! Don't tell me you don't read WebMama's!"

"Well, I'm not a mother and I haven't called anyone 'Mama' since I was about three, so..."

Harriet sighed. "I weary of your corrosive remarks." She flopped down on the couch the same way she had sprawled out across it many times at university.

"Ok, tell me about WebMama's," I said. It felt like it could be a long one so kicked off my shoes and stretched out beside her. At least it was a buffet, the food would keep warm for a bit.

And I was intrigued, I'd give her that, but I saw Allan and Dean deep in conversation and I wondered if they had realised the error of their ways. Allan dragged Dean off when he saw me looking, which was oddly assertive for him.

"I am never going to listen to WeddingWang123. Ever. Again," Harriet pouted as she put her head on my lap. I tried not to show my surprise but there was definitely a jump.

"We used to spend most Saturday mornings like this. The only difference is I don't have a sick bucket underneath me. Don't act so shocked," grumbled Harriet.

"I'm not shocked, I'm pleasantly surprised."

Harriet sniffed. "I long for the days of yore when my biggest problem was chundering into a bucket." I had forgotten her tendency to become melodramatic. "It was a simpler time," I confirmed. "No bills, no mortgages, no jobs-"

"No children," muttered Harriet.

"Harriet! You're pregnant?"

"No. And Sam, we're almost 30, you're not supposed to sound so horrified at the prospect. It's not like we are 16 and about to sit our GCSEs."

Harriet sat up and composed herself with a delicate dab at her eyes - the sort the Queen might do if she was allowed to show emotion.

"I have been trying to persuade Allan for quite some time now that it is...well, the time to have a child. In fact, I have been trying to persuade him for so long that I fear the time has passed." She flopped back against the sofa and raised a hand to her brow.

"Harriet, you're 29, not 69, and even then, I am pretty sure some crazy scientist would have a bash at artificially inseminating you."

Harriet gave me a 'don't be so disgusting' glare.

"It doesn't matter one jot. It's too late and I have dashed my chances." I was so bamboozled by all the old timey language that it took me a minute to remember the most pertinent question.

"So, you are becoming a barren old maid, I follow that bit, but where does WebMama's come in, and WeddingWank123?"

"It's WeddingWang123."

"I'm not sure that makes it much better."

There came that glare again.

"WeddingWang123 said her DH-"

"DH?"

"Darling Husband," now it was just a glare of general disgust, "...didn't want a baby, so she suggested a threesome."

I considered this series of events for a few moments. "Nope, I'm lost. Is the threesome some sort of consolation prize?"

Now the glare said, 'you are an abomination'.

"No! You suggest the threesome to put things in perspective," she said, almost adding an unladylike 'duh!'

I nodded politely, once again transported back to school days when I had absolutely no idea what was going on in Maths but too much of a people pleaser to let the teacher know.

"Oh no, you have your Maths face on," sighed Harriet. "It is meant to make them realise that they don't want anyone else, they want you."

"And a baby?"

"Exactly! "Harriet beamed as if I was the slow child in her class who had finally managed to spell 'dog'.

"What could go wrong?" I asked, although I knew the answer - everything.

"I know!" said Harriet. "But Allan is not your typical man," she continued, almost with pride. He seemed pretty typical to me - he had a job in middle management, watched a lot of documentaries about World War II and talked relentlessly about his company car.

"You'll never believe this, Sam. He said 'ok' to a threesome - then went back to browsing the car catalogue - he is due an upgrade of his company car, you know."

"Really?"

"Yes, it's going to have heated seats and it will also be a lovely teal colour. Anyway, I'm getting sidetracked."

I would have gone further than sidetracked, where we were was beyond any track, deep in the scary unexplored recesses of the forest of Harriet's subconscious, which was at first seemed like a well-pruned English country garden, but it was only camouflaging neurotic Vietcong with babies on the brain.

"So, he looked up very calmly from his car catalogue and said, "OK"."

"OK?"

"OK. And he can't understand why I am annoyed at him," she threw her hands up.

"Really? After he agreed to something you suggested. He must be insane."

If Harriet had the power to send me away to think about what I had done, she would have. Luckily for her, Dean appeared to escort me into the dinner hall. I leapt up, determined not to miss out on the buffet this time around.

"Let's talk about this later, Harriet. I'm sure it will all work out," I said as Dean pulled me towards the dinner like he was a speedboat and I was one of those rubber donut rings they pull behind them.

I noticed Dean kept looking back at Harriet nervously, not that I blamed him. She was glaring at Allan the way disgruntled animals look at you in the zoo.

"I have just had an interesting conversation with Allan. It was crazy," Dean whispered in my ear as we joined Paxton and Nicky at our table, who were already getting stuck into tempting platefuls of food.

I let out a loud laugh. "That's a good one! I didn't know you had such a wicked sense of humour, Dean."

"What did he say?' asked Paxton, spearing a bit of swordfish with his fork.

"He just said he had an interesting conversation with Allan!" I said, still laughing a little.

Paxton almost choked on his fish and banged the table in delight. Nicky hooted and applauded.

"That is a good one, Dean," said Paxton, once he had recovered his composure.

"The only person I have met that was more boring than Allan was..." Nicky said, trailing off into thought. "Oh God, I can't actually think of anyone!" I wondered if hell had frozen over, I expected she would at least have claimed to have met a Tibetan monk who had taken a vow of boredom.

Luckily, normality was restored when Harriet and Allan shuffled in and took their seats. We all managed to compose ourselves after Dean's joke, just about. Despite a few titters, we said our hellos and Paxton launched into one of his ribald tales.

"I say, Dean, let me tell you about the time I slept with my mother!"

Dean had been buttering a bit of crusty bread, but suddenly went very still.

"Don't worry, it's not as bad as it seems," I said. "Dean doesn't know about 'Family Halls'."

"Senior Students in Halls take on extra responsibility. There is always one male and one female per floor. They are there to organise events, help with the administration and provide advice to the younger students," explained Harriet. "So they form a family unit. You have the husband and the wife, then you have the children, don't you, Allan?" her voice rising to a kettle whistle by the end of the sentence.

This was going to be a long evening.

Chapter 23

About fifteen minutes later, we had all filed back to the table with our plates of food. It was only then I really noticed the two empty seats beside me. June was supposed to be joining us, and it was traditional at St Fillan's reunions for a member of staff to sit at each table as a guest. I leaned over and flipped the place card over to see who it would be, though I had a funny feeling that I already knew.

"Professor P - I should have known," I said, showing it to Dean.

"Oh, are him and June having a bit of a thing? She said something about having drinks with him last night," said Dean, tucking a napkin in to protect his piano tie.

"I think they might be, and God forbid that tie should become even more of a mess, eh?" I said, threatening it with a dripping clump of pheasant curry, which made him recoil.

"I think it's a very nice tie, Dean. You look incredibly handsome in it," piped up Allan from across the table. It was a strange thing for him to say; the greatest compliment he had ever given was that Harriet's wedding dress was 'weather appropriate'.

In fact, Harriet stopped short of putting a spoonful of curry in her mouth and looked askance at him. Dean avoided eye contact and nervously flattened out his napkin-bib so it covered all of the tie. Paxton, Nicky and I all exchanged puzzled glances but shrugged, with the unspoken assumption that Allan had imbibed a little too much of the complimentary 'champagne'.

I heard giggling behind us and turned to see June and Professor P finally joining the party.

"Oh, you're our staff rep, Prof! Take a seat!" said Paxton, raising a glass. It was actually Harriet's, not his, and she snatched it off him.

"Sorry Hazza, mea culpa," said Paxton, locating his own slightly to the left.

"Apology accepted, Paxton," said Harriet. "It's really not a big deal. I really need something bigger, anyway." With that, she grabbed an almost-full bottle of Chardonnay and began to chug the whole thing. Most of us watched in a mixture of admiration and concern. Paxton just started chanting 'Down it! Down it!" and applauded her when she polished it off.

"Thank you. I just thought, why not?" She said, dabbing her lips. "It's not as if there are any reasons why I shouldn't be drinking wine right now, are there, Allan?"

"No, dear," said Allan, concentrating on his plate. "You should speak to Dean, actually. He knows a lot about wine, he might be able to give you some pointers." He looked up and gave Dean a coy smile.

There was a definite twitch smouldering away in Harriet's eye now. Dean laughed, but thinly, like a watered-down wine being poured down the drain.

"Have you all met June?" I blurted. I felt like a tour guide trying to distract a bus load of holidaymakers from a fiery car crash.

There were various murmurs of 'not properly', 'only briefly' and 'I don't think so' from the majority of the table.

"Well, she is very enchanting," said Professor P, kissing her hand. "I am very lucky I was assigned this table, and indeed, this seat, right next to her."

"Yes, it really is quite the coincidence," I said. Dean sniggered much more heartily than he did at Allan's compliment.

"Your shoulders look tense, Sam. Let me help you," said June, clamping them in a painful pincer move.

"Ow! Fine, I'll behave" I said, dropping my cutlery. "As you can see, June is an expert masseuse. She's a friend of mine from Edinburgh and she fancied a break in St Fillan's for the weekend."

Now everyone did a variety of 'oohs', 'ahs', 'not at alls' and 'nice to meet yous'. I quickly introduced each of the St Fillan's crew in turn to June, and I could see her trying not to smile too much as she remembered all the stories I had told her over the years about each of them.

"I hope you don't mind me gate-crashing the reunion. Sam just made the town sound so nice, I jumped at the chance to come up," she said, giving me a reassuring but discreet thumbs up at her side.

"This woman is an absolute powerhouse," said Professor P with a knowing chuckle, but I knew I looked like I had tasted something sour. What he said about June was true, but I really could have done without one of his sexual innuendos while eating. "She knows more about cultural capital than Bourdieu himself. I think she could teach me a few things," he said, but this time much more genuinely. Could it be, Professor P admired a woman for more than her ability to look good in one of those Britney Spears school uniforms?

"She really is simply the best," I said, smiling at June. "Like Tina Turner, but with a Masters degree and an unbending desire to destroy capitalism."

"Welcome, June. I'm Paxton. I hope you'll spare me from the guillotine, when the time comes," said Paxton.

"Well, I would imagine eating the rich is very filling, so I might let you go. Depends how hungry I am," said June, skewering a chunk of meat on her plate with a smile. Paxton loved it and applauded, while Professor P might as well have had those cartoon lovehearts jumping out of his eyes.

"Human meat may be taboo, but it is very delicious," said Nicky, and everyone sighed heavily and pushed their plates away. "Or so I was told by one of my Central American drug gang contacts."

"So is it all round to yours for liver, fava beans and a nice Chianti after this, Nicky? What's for dessert? A line of cocaine?" June said, offering me a fist bump under the table. If I had said it, it would have been dripping with exasperation and sarcasm, but she said it in such a lighthearted and good-humoured way that all Nicky could do was laugh along with everyone else to try and save some face.

"And you're funny to boot! You certainly have very talented friends, Sam," said Nicky, making sure to bat her eyelashes at Dean, just in case he felt a bit neglected.

He smiled a little, obviously not as averse to her attentions as Allan's, but remained professional, rubbing my arm with his hand.

"I have got a fun game we can play!" announced Paxton. "Inspired by Nicky's adventures. If you had to eat someone else at the table, who would it be?"

"Dean," said Allan, a little too quickly and enthusiastically. "He looks delicious, don't you think, dear?" He gave Harriet a wide grin and she looked around as if she had just been beamed onto a spaceship. Dean muttered something about God helping him or striking him down, it was hard to make out. Paxton looked at Dean and licked his lips while laughing hysterically. Nicky looked deep in concentration, as if she was trying to come up with a story about cannibalism that was somehow both a bit sexy and in good taste.

Meanwhile, the cogs were beginning to turn in my head. Why was Allan being so complimentary of Dean? It was starting to verge on obscene. It was like he wanted to have sex with him or something. Then I remembered the conversation Harriet told me about, the one where she had proposed a threesome and it had backfired. Right after that, Dean and Allan were deep in conversation. Could it be that he was trying to lure Dean into their boudoir? I put a hand to my mouth, in shock, but also trying to stop myself from laughing. I couldn't be 100% sure though, so I decided to wait it out a little, to see if I was right, but also just for entertainment value.

"Cannibalism is supposed to be one of the universal taboos, but trust a table of St Fillan's graduates to make it their main topic of dinner conversation," shrugged Professor P, pouring himself and June more wine. "You're going to need it," he told her. "Imagine having to teach entire classes of these people. It's no wonder they give me a loyalty discount at the wine shop."

"Ha! You and Sam should swap tips. She knows her wine, but so does Dean. I mean, they both do, he works in a wine shop. It's how they met, after all," June said. She knew she had messed up though, and you could see alarm in her eyes, even as the last words fell out of her mouth.

"I thought Dean was an actor?" said Harriet, as quick as a snake eating some cute baby animal in a nature documentary.

"Oh, I am," said Dean coolly. "I was doing research for a part. I take my craft very seriously."

"I bet you do," said Allan, far too excitedly. I caught Dean's eye and knew I was right - Allan was trying to get Dean to be the third partner in the ménage à trois Harriet had insisted upon but didn't actually want. It was time to pull the plug, it was more merciful, if less fun.

"Dean, let's go for a smoke," I said, wracking my brains for any reason to leave the dining room.

"You don't smoke," said Harriet, quick on the draw again.

"I hear all the cool kids are doing it. You know me, always got to be in the It crowd," I said, dragging Dean towards the door and past the actual socialites from our year, who looked morally offended by the association.

Chapter 24

I only realised how ashen-faced Dean had become when we were outside in the dark, his ghostly face making him look like he was in a black and white movie.

"You know how I was talking to Allan at the bar?" he said, gulping as if he had just been given some terrible terminal diagnosis.

"Yes?"

"I think he wants to have sex with me," he said gravely.

"Oh," I said, feigning surprise.

"Or maybe it's Harriet. Or both of them. I'm not very sure. Maybe I am having a terrible nightmare and need to be analysed by Freud?"

I tried not to laugh, I really did. But it happened.

"This is no laughing matter, Sam!" Dean gasped.

"I'm sorry. I had a little chat with Harriet too, you see."

Dean slid behind a column at the sound of her name and mouthed 'Can she see me?'

"It's all a big misunderstanding. Sort of."

"They don't want to have sex with me?" He edged out a little from behind the column but did not commit fully to the endeavour.

"Well, I can't speak for Allan, but I don't think it was Harriet's original intention."

"I'm confused, but they seem pretty mixed up too," said Dean.

We both smiled a little and Dean seemed to relax - his eyes rested on me and didn't dart at the sound of loud noises for a change, which I can only presume he thought was Allan commencing a mating call. A little voice inside my head, impulsive and shrill, told me to smile back. It was odd, it wasn't the same little voice I was used to, the one that told me I looked crap in shorts, or that everyone could tell I had just picked a spot on my face in the bathroom, or that sending Christmas cards to wine shops was weird. No, it was almost a positive voice, like a fairground announcer telling you this would be the ride of your life, or an advert on the radio that almost makes you believe you need a new bathroom.

"We've worked out what you're up to," said Harriet, appearing in front of us, silhouetted in the entryway like a film noir detective, Allan shuffling into frame shortly afterwards. I had only managed a half smile by this point, and the little voice in my head had told me that I probably looked like Sylvester Stallone trying to smile after a particularly bad round in one of the Rocky films.

"Look Harriet, I'm not going to have sex with you. Or Allan. Or a combination of you and Allan," snapped Dean. A group of guys who happened to be vaping outside, all of whom I am sure now work in Canary Wharf and make me want to sing the Internationale whenever I see them in their shiny suits, looked on with a mixture of shock and acceptance, like they had been on the receiving end of that conversation many times themselves.

"Well, it's not like you'll be having sex with Sam either," said Harriet with a sassiness that I thought had died long ago.

"What do you mean?" I bristled.

"This is all some sort of arrangement between the two of you," she said shrewdly, then she gave Allan a nudge. He tried to scowl too, but he just looked like he was blaming a fart on someone else.

"Something's just not seemed right since the beginning," continued our Columbo.

"There were no photos of you two on social media, then there were hundreds. And Dean appeared in your life all of a sudden, very conveniently. Almost too conveniently. And June let it slip about the wine shop."

"You and Allan clearly have very active imaginations. Perhaps you should channel it into your own bedroom activities instead of gawking at ours," I said, acting as spokesperson for both Dean and me. My comrade stood behind me lest Allan or Harriet make a lust-filled lunge for him.

With that, I turned, my nose in the air, and retreated to my bedroom. Dean faithfully scuttled behind me, but then I heard more footsteps – apparently we had developed quite a following.

Harriet was dragging Allan along the corridor like some over-sized luggage.

"Are you seriously following us?" I asked.

"I'm right, I know I'm right and nothing you can say will convince me otherwise!" stomped Harriet.

"You hear that a lot, don't you?" I said sympathetically to Allan. Dean sniggered. "Follow us if you want, I'm not sure what you expect to happen. It's not the medieval monarchy, we aren't going to have a 'bedding' ceremony and sell tickets on the door."

"You kinky freaks," chimed in Dean.

Harriet and I both huffed and we set off down the corridor once more. I seized Dean's hand and he wrapped his fingers around mine. I didn't have time to digest or analyse it though, so consumed was I with proving Harriet wrong, even if she was very right.

Soon we reached our room and stood there as an awkward foursome.

"We're going in now," I announced as if this was a production for the visually impaired.

"Go on then," said Harriet.

"I'm putting my key in the door," I continued.

Allan and Harriet huddled in closer to check I actually was and perhaps block my way should I make a run for it. Instead, I surprised even myself by taking a deep breath and plunging through the door, pulling Dean in with me. He must have been shocked too as he let out a gasp as the door slammed behind us.

Chapter 25

"Are you sure you two don't want to come in?" I called through the door a few minutes later. "We can make it a foursome, or is that one too many for you?"

I heard Harriet give an indignant gasp on the other side of the door.

"I don't understand, dear, are we having a threesome or not?" asked the poor, clueless Allan.

Harriet shooshed him. I laughed and Dean mumbled some terrified excuses and locked himself in the bathroom.

I heard more footsteps in the corridor with the rhythm of a jaunty river dance rather than a walk.

"Harriet! Allan! What the hell happened back there? Has Allan turned gay? Finally, something interesting about him. Sorry, Allan" called Paxton, who was now humming a ditty to accompany his dance.

"Paxton!" I shouted and banged on the door. "Save us from them! They're sexual predators!"

I could see Harriet turning bright red with rage through the peephole. "Allan is just a bit confused, Paxton. Don't listen to her. She is the one hiding something. I don't even think Sam and Dean are really a couple!"

Paxton let out a gasp. "Really, you think so?"

"Yes!"

"Well, why don't the three of us retire to my room and you can get me up to speed on this very shocking turn of events," he said, beginning to lead them off.

"It all started with these photos on Facebook, you see," I heard Harriet say as her voice trailed down the corridor.

"Is it safe to come out?" asked Dean from behind the bathroom door.

"The coast is clear," I replied, beginning to feel the dress' halterneck dig into me. I had forgotten it had about a four-hour window before it turned into a torture device. Next would be the zip somehow tightening until it was a 19th Century corset.

"I need to get out of this thing," I said, fishing my Bananas in Pyjamas shorts and t-shirt set out from behind my pillow and heading for the now vacant bathroom. The thought of asking Dean to help me out of the dress did pass through my mind, a way to test if I would like him to help me out of my clothes for less practical reasons. I was tired though, the dinner had used up all my energy, and I was 29, not 19, and this was reality, not a scene in a trashy romantic movie.

In fact, once I was in the bathroom, I didn't want to come out. It felt like a safe haven from all the craziness outside, its cool tiled walls an extra barrier between me and the outside world, the reassuring hum of the extractor fan a welcome change from Harriet shouting through the door.

Then a knock disturbed my quiet space.

"You've not done an Elvis and died on the toilet, have you?" asked Dean.

I sighed heavily and finished taking off my make-up. "Still alive! Out in a minute."

"I'm not going to die on the toilet at this reunion. Can you imagine the years of gossip Harriet would get out of that?" I said, leaving the bathroom to see Dean had followed my lead and slipped into something more comfortable - an old purple t-shirt with a rip at the neck, emblazoned with 'Drama Camp Leader 2013' and a pair of boxers with Marlon Brando's face all over them. How I would control myself, I wasn't sure.

"Bananas in Pyjamas?" he asked, giving me a sidelong look from across the room.

"Marlon Brando boxers? You come to me, on the day of my university reunion, dressed in novelty underwear?" I said, doing my best Godfather impression.

"Touché," said Dean, lying back on his bed. He let out a long breath. "That was certainly a very interesting evening. Your friends are absolutely mad, you know."

"We had to make our own entertainment back in the day. There wasn't much nightlife here. I think the only way not to go completely mad was to be completely mad, if that makes sense. It appears some things never change," I said, flopping down on my own mattress.

"What was the story with Harriet and Allan, then?" asked Dean, a little hesitantly.

"Oh, Harriet wants to have a baby, so she tried to make Allan get on board with her plan by suggesting a threesome she doesn't actually want." Dean scrunched up his face in confusion. "Don't ask me, she read it on the internet. She thought it would make him realise how much he loved her. It sounds like he got the wrong end of the stick and tried to recruit you."

I am not sure which one of us started laughing first, but soon we were both in the grips of that hysterical laughter that you can only reach when you are past the point of exhaustion and have entered some sort of nirvana of insanity.

Dean was the first to regain some composure. Then he looked at his phone. "Sweet Jesus! It's only 9.30pm!" This only set him off again. Between increasingly asthmatic cackles, he managed to say, "How can these people fuck up a night so quickly? This is shit that that would go down at 3am anywhere else!"

I felt tears starting to roll down my face as I howled with laughter. "It's almost a talent, isn't it?" I said, followed by a helpless squeal.

Eventually we regained some composure and managed to go as much as perhaps 10 or 15 seconds without laughing. "What shall we do with the rest of the night, then?" asked Dean, getting up off the bed to look out the window.

"All the pubs will be closed in an hour or two, and I don't really fancy going back down the stairs now I'm in my Bananas in Pyjamas ensemble," I said, wondering where he was going with this, and where I was too, essentially confining us to the room in state of semi-undress for the evening.

"Good point, it might be too erotic for them to cope with," said Dean, glancing back from the window.

"That's about as amusing as your tragic underpants," I said, getting up to put away my dress, which I had brought back from the bathroom in a crumpled heap.

"Yeah, yeah, whatever," he said, picking up his bag and walking back over to his bed. "That's enough of that, smart Alec. Any ideas of what we could get up to?"

My back was turned as I was hanging my dress up in the closet - I hadn't kept it in good condition all these years by letting it lie on the floor. "I don't know. If we hurry, we can probably catch the weather on one of the rolling news channels." The damn halterneck kept slipping off the hanger and I was starting to get frustrated.

"Or we could have sex?" said Dean.

The dress dropped out my hands and onto the floor. I left it there and began to stammer a reply: "Er...are you...I mean, I...really?"

The thought had been dancing around at the back of my head, I could admit that (to myself), but this all seemed a bit sudden and in your face.

I took a deep breath and turned around, not sure what I was expecting to see, maybe the boxers cast aside and Dean reclining on the bed with a rose between his teeth?

What I did see was Dean sitting on his bed with a bottle of wine in his hands. The label read, 'Sex' in a scrawl and was decorated with equally crude graffiti-style penises and breasts.

"You should have seen your face!" hooted Dean, falling back on his bed.

"Oh my God, what even is that?" I said, affecting a carefree laugh and going over to take a closer look.

"The marketers at Head Office are calling it the sequel to the I'm Sorry Rosé."

I took the bottle off him to get a better look. Divine Drinks had really excelled themselves with this one; the bottle even had a distinctly phallic shape to it.

The wine itself promised to be much nicer than the Rosé, not that that would be hard.

Short of actually causing seizures, it would be difficult to be worse than that one. It was a dark red Italian Primitivo, the sort of wine you immediately imagine lusty farmhands and curvaceous milkmaids helping to harvest and crushing the grapes with their bare feet in one of those big barrels.

"Go on, let's have some sex, then," I said, tearing off the foil wrapper. "Have you got a corkscrew?"

"I always come prepared!" said Dean, producing one from his bag and handing it to me. He might have the same taste in underwear as a camp Mafia henchman, but not every guy on the street had the endurance to keep innuendos going this long, I thought as I worked the screw into the cork.

"Let me," he said, holding out his hands. I decided to let him open it. After all, think of the hilarious photo opportunities of him manhandling a penis-shaped bottle, and he did do this for a living.

Fittingly, he slid the cork out in a business-like fashion and picked up two of those standard-issue hotel-room glasses from the bureau with a flourish.

He poured the wine into the glasses and the colour was as rich as it looked in the bottle. If the watery pink I'm Sorry Rosé and the Sex were lined up next to each other, they would like the before and after on a makeover show.

Dean handed me my glass while he swirled and took a deep sniff. "Notice the aromas of tobacco and chocolate, characteristic of the Primitivo grape, or, as it is known in the States, Zinfandel."

"Dean?"

"Yes?"

"You're off duty, you can just knock it back. Although you're right, it does smell good."

"Cheers!" we said in unison, clinking our glasses.

After a sip, we both fell back into our separate beds with satisfied sighs.

"Wow," said Dean.

"Yeah, wow. This is good stuff." I almost felt like fanning myself, I could already feel that warm wine feeling creeping over me. "It tastes like the love child of a fancy dark chocolate impulse buy and, I imagine, one of those mythical Cuban cigars rolled on some poor hard-working virgin's thighs." I took another sip and whirled my glass thoughtfully. 'In fact, I think the marketers missed a trick. Better Than Sex is by far a more suitable name."

"Oh, I wouldn't know. I spend my summers as an innocent virgin cigar roller in Havana," said Dean, coyly hiding behind his glass.

"Ok," I laughed. "I'll admit, it's been a while, so I might be off base with that evaluation." I allowed myself an extra-large glug of the stuff. "But daaamn!"

"It's a very good wine," admitted Dean, holding it up to the light the way fancy wine people do. "But maybe you should refresh your memory before committing to such a pronouncement."

He looked at me out of the corner of his eye and I immediately peered into the depths of my glass, occasionally giving it a little shake like it was a Magic 8 Ball that would answer questions like, 'Did Dean seriously just say that?' 'Does he really want to have sex with me or is this another bit of witty repartee?' and 'Is this actually happening or am I in a coma from the I'm Sorry Rosé and this has all been a dream?'

"Are you claiming to be better in bed than this wine is? Because drinking a good red in your Bananas in Pyjamas PJs after a long hard day is pretty hard to beat," I said, following up with a loud breezy laugh in case it was all just a massive joke that I hadn't got.

Dean laughed too, but it wasn't as big as mine. "All I'm saying is that I'm over here if you need me," he said with a shrug and turned on the TV. I watched what appeared to be the eternal weather report for a few seconds, until it once again told me it was 32 degrees in Dakar, and I couldn't take it anymore. Was I really just going to sit here and watch the weather of the world for the umpteenth time this weekend, when there was an apparently willing man next to me, even if he was wearing those hideous boxer shorts?

So I got up, tried to dislodge the wedgie my PJ shorts had created as elegantly as possible, walked across the room, feeling as nervous as an actor on stage on opening night, took the remote from his bedside table and switched the screen off.

"Hey! They were just about to tell us the temperature in Brazzaville!" said Dean.

"Urgh fine, if you're going to be like that, I'm going back to bed," I said, starting to scurry back across. It had taken all the courage I had to get this far, plus whatever Dutch courage the wine had gifted me. It was just a joke too far.

I felt something catch the waistband of my shorts and turned back around. Dean had caught them, and they were now stretched out like those giant clown trousers. "Oi, you absolute Banana in Pyjamas, get into bed. Of course Brazzaville can wait."

I followed in the wake of my elasticated shorts, feeling this was some sort of vindication for always refusing to buy sexy underwear. I smiled, knowing I had clearly been right all along.

"What are you smiling about?" said Dean, pulling me down onto the bed and kissing me, but he was smiling too, I could feel it.

"Well, who knew Bananas in Pyjamas were such an aphrodisiac?" I said between kisses. I pulled away, but put my arms around his neck. "Imagine if I had trussed myself up in some barely-there thong, I would have looked and felt like an overstuffed sausage for nothing."

"What an image," he said. I pulled his shirt off by the handy rip at the collar.

"Sorry, especially when you made such an effort," I said, holding the tattered thing at arm's length and letting it drop to the floor.

"I do feel like I owe you more," he said, slipping one arm out of my t-shirt.

"Owe me?" I said, pulling back, my arm half sticking out the bottom of my top.

"It's what I signed up for, right?' said Dean, pulling me back in, but I pushed him away.

"Sorry, I thought that would sound sexier than it did," he said, trying to reel me back in by the shorts, but I let the elastic snap back against me.

"Is this all just some sort of sex version of a package holiday to you? Because you felt sorry for me?" I said, taking a step out of the bed and out of his range.

Dean didn't say anything, which was approximately 250,000 times worse than if he had said something, short of confessing to being a wanted criminal.

"Oh God," I said, pulling my pyjama top back down and retreating to my bed. I sat down on it and pulled my knees up. Dean just looked at me.

"I don't know, okay?" he said, like he had been asked why he liked the divisive ham and pineapple pizza. "I thought I was doing you a favour, but then there were times, where, I don't know, I thought we were helping each other. I guess I just wanted to find out."

But he had resigned himself to never knowing, there was something in the way he pulled his t-shirt back on. "I'm going to go for a walk," he said, slipping his suit trousers back on.

I thought about saying something that would make him stay, but I wanted to make him pay for what he had said.

Dean turned the door handle. "I'm sorry, if that means anything. I really am," he said, without turning around, like he was rehearsing for something else.

Chapter 26

Dean didn't come back that night. I didn't think he would, so I took the liberty of consoling myself with the rest of the bottle of wine and a couple of the tiny gins in the mini bar. I thought about messaging June or Paxton, but I really just wanted to have (a bottle of) sex by myself and wait until the initial wave of embarrassment about the whole thing passed.

After snoozing the alarm several times, it was a knock at the door which finally woke me up. I could only presume it was the cleaners starting their daily rounds, or Harriet returning to check in on us. Dread brewed in my stomach as I rolled out of bed to answer it.

Relief whooshed over me when I saw a dishevelled Paxton at the door in last night's clothes.

"Oh my God, Sam, you won't believe the night I had," he said striding through the door. "I had to come and tell you and Dean right away. Where is Deano, anyway?"

"Oh, he has gone for breakfast already," I said. I realised that I didn't actually know where Dean was. He could have wandered down towards the beach and fallen off the cliffs for all I knew. It wouldn't have been the first time a night out had ended like that for some poor soul in St Fillan's. I mean, realistically he had probably just ended up in the bar and kipped on Harriet's old reliable sofa, but still.

"I can tell you're lying, but I've not got time for that right now. I need to tell you what happened last night," Paxton said, leaping onto Dean's bed and bouncing around.

"What happened?" I asked, looking out the window towards the foamy white high tide stretching along the beach, as if Dean's bloated corpse was about to appear in the waves, unsure just exactly how I felt about that.

"Whatever you're brooding about, stop it right now. I demand it," said Paxton, leaping from the bed and banging his fist on the bedside table.

"Fine! Tell me." I sighed.

"I just spent the night in Harriet and Allan's room," he said, opening up his arms as if he expected an applause.

"And?"

"What do you mean, 'and'?" said Paxton, shoving me in the arm.

"It's no big deal, we spent most of uni sleeping over in each other's rooms," I said.

"Yeah, but this was different. They said you knew about their little misunderstanding with Dean," said Paxton, trailing off with a wiggle of his eyebrows.

Had he done something with them in Dean's absence? "Oh God. You didn't, did you?"

"Indeed I did!" he said, puffing out his chest. "I had a threesome with Harriet and Allan Benson. That's one to tick off the bucket list. I tell you, I take it all back about Allan being boring-"

"Please stop talking! This is like being given a pop-out picture book of your parents having sex. I don't need to know the gory details," I said, sticking my fingers in my ears.

"Too bad - you're going to get them. I'll find you at breakfast and tell you all about it then," threatened Paxton.

He left the room and walked down the corridor. I went to shut the door behind him and saw him rap on Allan and Harriet's door. "Call me, you nymphos!" he bellowed. A scandalised squeak came from the other side of the flimsy door.

I quickly got changed out of my Bananas in Pyjamas ensemble, unsure if I would ever be able to wear the innocent garments again; it wasn't their fault they had played a part in my embarrassing rejection. I settled on a denim skirt and smart V-neck top, to give everyone the very false impression that I wasn't the sort of person who lived in leggings and hoodies at the weekend. Suitably attired,

I headed down for breakfast, wondering if I would find Dean there. I hoped I wouldn't, I was tired of the act, especially after last night.

Down in the dining hall, Nicky was in full voice.

"Then I used the Krav Maga I learnt with the IDF to drop kick the mugger into the bushes. Last night was just so crazy." An attentive waiter nodded eagerly but the group of alumni around prodded their muesli unenthusiastically. She spied me coming closer and I let out an involuntary groan.

"Sam!" she called, waving her arms like one of those inflatable wavy arm men. I definitely wasn't going to get away with just ignoring her. The man sitting next to her saw his chance to escape and seized it, making for the breakfast buffet like a soldier under enemy fire. "Have you seen Dean?"

"He's somewhere around here," I said, looking around to see if I could indeed see him.

"Why?"

"I need to talk to Dean about my company, sweetie," she replied. "I gave him my card, remember?" Now the tone approached that which you would use on an elderly relative who keeps asking if the Germans are still bombing us.

"Yeah, sure," I said, still looking around for him. Paxton's voice distracted me though, but I turned to see him loudly describing his evening's adventures to none other than Dean. My heart sunk twice, first at seeing Dean, then hearing the loud and vivid description of Paxton's night, the phrases 'makeshift sex swing' and 'ways to use a loofah' cropping up.

Thankfully, Paxton broke off when he saw me and waved. "Oh, I promised to tell Sam all this too, let's go over," he said, dragging Dean to our table. He looked a little green around the gills, was it because he had to face me, or was is because he had had to listen to Paxton?

"Dean! Just the person I was looking for!" said Nicky as they reached the table. Dean looked at his shoes, or at least I think he did, I could only see him out of the corner of my eye because I was staring at the table.

Nicky jumped up and shot an arm through Dean's folded ones. "Come on handsome, let's go talk business!" she declared, marching him off to the foyer, the clip-clop of her high-heeled shoes having a certain jackboot ring to them.

June appeared at my side and clutched my arm. "Who is that walking embodiment of a narcissistic personality disorder? I would love to study her if she wasn't so obnoxious."

"You're very perceptive," I replied. "Normally it takes people an entire month to work it out."

"Try a few hours," June grabbed her cutlery whilst staring daggers at Nicky. "I'm not being big-headed. I saw her go to bed at 10pm with a cup of hot chocolate. Her room was right next to Professor P's."

"Excuse me, ladies, I was about to tell Sam about my evening," said Paxton, muscling his way in between us.

"Go and get yourself a coffee and come back in five minutes. You, Harriet and Allan were looking very cosy last night, I don't want to hear about what you got up to while I'm eating," said June, waving him off. Paxton pouted but dutifully headed over to the coffee machine.

"And what were you doing in Professor P's room?" I asked once Paxton had plodded off.

June adopted an unflappable expression, the same one she used when a muscular demi-god client walked into her parlour.

"He was showing me his slides of the Turgu tribe's spring festival."

"Is he still using that line?" I laughed. "I thought he would have mixed it up by now."

June dissolved into jelly. "Oh Sam, I know it's wrong and he is corny and ageing disgracefully but I just can't help myself. It's probably some ingrained colonial self sabotage but I don't care."

Professor P winked at us from the breakfast buffet.

"He says he can wangle me a place as an assistant researcher on his next trip to Bhutan in a few weeks," June said, returning his wink. "I could be a real-life researcher with an academic sex machine," she added with a lick of her lip, but I knew she wasn't really talking to me at all anymore.

"That sounds great," I said, poking at the cereal dispenser in front of me.

June slowly descended from Planet Professor P. "What about you? Rumour has it you had yourself some fun too last night."

“Not as much as Harriet and Allan...and Paxton,” I deflected.

“I said, not while I’m eating,” June groaned, putting down her knife and fork. “But who would have thought - they seem so utterly and completely beige,” she said, unable to resist the juicy morsel of gossip.

“Well it certainly sounds as if er...Paxton brought a splash of colour to their lives.”

Just then Harriet and Allan entered the hall looking more loved-up than they had ever done before. Her crimson cheeks contrasted nicely with the darkly satisfied circles around his eyes.

Soon the gaze of the entire room was on them. It seemed that all around me people were transforming and changing, so it was nice to see that you could always rely on the constant of the university rumour mill.

Harriet grabbed a sheepish Allan’s hand, put on her best ‘celebrity on a talk show’ smile and dragged him to a table in the centre of the room. She smiled at her table mates, who studied her as eagerly as if she was a gossip column hot off the press. I could tell I was keeping June from having full-on eye sex with Professor P so slunk off to get the latest on our threesome twosome. It would at least be interesting to compare and contrast their story with Paxton’s, when I eventually heard it.

The seats on either side of Harriet and Allan remained vacant, probably because their former classmates didn’t want to be the next to be propositioned.

“You’re looking very...satisfied,” I said as I sat down.

Harriet’s teeth gleamed in a broad smile and Allan sniggered like a naughty schoolboy. “Allan and I have just had a blazing row,” purred Harriet.

“Oh?” I crunched on my cornflakes.

“Yes, I think our little experiment has brought some passion back into our lives,” she declared. Allan nodded meekly. “That’s...great, I think?” I replied.

“Oh, it is, Sam, it is. And we owe it all to Paxton, we really do,” continued Harriet, obviously imagining herself in an Oscar acceptance speech scenario.

“Allan was completely incensed. Like a wild animal,” said Harriet. Allan nodded dutifully.

I must have looked unconvinced, because she added, "You'd never know it to look at him, but he is quite a tiger behind closed doors."

"Is that true?" I asked as Allan leafed through a Sunday supplement on car maintenance he must have found in the lobby.

"Oh, it is," she gushed, stirring heaps of berry compote into a thick yoghurt. She beckoned me closer and lowered her voice, "We had...fun last night, don't get me wrong, but Allan told me that he never wants to share me with anyone ever again. After all, he said, I am going to be the mother of his children."

"Wow," was all I could really manage.

"Wow indeed," smiled Harriet.

"I definitely feel it has reignited the spark," she decreed. "Haven't we, Allan?"

"Yes dear," he mumbled as he puzzled over 4 down in a crossword puzzle.

Harriet wasn't quite finished. "Flaming rows, screaming matches, broken china and fiery embraces..."

"Looks like the baby won't be the only one screaming and crying in your household," I muttered.

"What was that?" Harriet asked while dreamily staring at Allan.

"4 down - wine - alternative name for Primitivo - 9 letters," Allan babbled to himself.

"Zinfandel," I said, joined by a voice behind me. Dean fidgeted with the back of my chair.

"Yes, that fits!" said Allan while Harriet playfully twisted his earlobe.

Dean didn't look like someone who had found the answer, though.

"Can we go and have a chat?" he said, the way doctors do just before they tell you that you have cancer.

"Of course," I replied with the faux breeziness of the patient who knew their death sentence was to be confirmed.

Harriet's view from Cloud 9 was obviously obscured as she giggled playfully and winked. "Go get him! There's no doubt about you two!"

I managed a noise halfway between vague agreement and a throat infection. I pushed my chair away and followed my gloomy executioner to the garden. It made me think of the sort of commandeered country gardens they killed deserters in during World War I. At least the flowers were pretty, even if your brain or heart was about to be spattered across the lovely roses.

"Don't look so glum," Dean said with a weak laugh. "There's nothing to worry about."

"You might have put in a convincing performance as my boyfriend, but you're not that good an actor." I leaned against the wall and considered drawing a bullseye over my heart.

Suddenly I had that sinking feeling we all get from time to time – when you are finishing an exam question and realise you misunderstood the whole thing, or you've blown an interview with an ill-advised joke about Brexit; the show is over, but you had so much more to give.

Dean gave one of those frustrated sighs you cannot fake. I had previously only seen it in divorced parents having to exchange their precious bundles for the weekend.

"Why are you making this so difficult?" he grumbled.

"Pardon me, is there a chopping block that you'd like me to put my head on for you?"

His foot nudged a stone on the ground.

"You know, I never actually expected you to have feelings for me." I felt my voice shake with emotion that I hadn't known I felt. "But I did expect you to have feelings in general. I know I'm just that sad lady from the wine shop to you, but you could treat me with a little respect and be straight with me."

Dean sighed again. I felt my breath falter. "You know what, consider yourself off duty. You've played your part. Exit, preferably pursued by a bear, but I don't think I'll have that much luck."

With that I walked through the dining room without looking back, trying my best to keep my head above the crowd, in case I drowned in the waves of something I felt building inside of me.

When I got to the safety of the corridor, I began to feel body and soul re-establish their respectful distance from each other.

I looked at a picture of a sailboat in a bland blue sea and marvelled at the swell of emotion that had come over me. I hadn't felt anything that intense since Sam and Diane didn't get together in Cheers, or when the wine shop finally ran out of that really nice Pinot Gris. Never forgive or forget.

I calmed myself with the thought that all this was about as real as a sitcom, a fact which itself promptly re-upset me. I saw Nicky coming out of the dining hall and towards us in the lobby, so tried to compose myself.

"I hope you haven't taken it all too badly?" Nicky said with robotic inflection of concern.

I tried to work out what she thought I was taking badly but most of my brain power was devoted to the dread of how she would broadcast this lovers' tiff; a few sniffles would probably become her talking me off a window ledge or stemming the blood flow from my freshly slashed wrists.

"It's a great opportunity."

I nodded automatically, like when you haven't heard someone properly and it would be too socially awkward to ask them to repeat themselves.

"He just did so well this weekend, but I'm a professional, I know the signs."

I sighed. I had never been one to indulge Nicky's flights of fancy.

"Sorry, what are you, a professional fantasist?"

Nicky cackled for the benefit of an imaginary audience.

"I suppose I am, in a sense. I create fantasies for other people." None more elaborate than the one you have fashioned for yourself, I thought. Nicky raised her eyebrows. I would say I barely contained my disgust, but she would say she divined my emotions thanks to a telepathic gift her gypsy grandmother passed down to her.

"I know what you are thinking." Apparently I was right. "Nicky is a total fantasist.' And maybe I am. Or maybe I am just a double agent for the Namibian government, you'll never really know."

And neither will you, I thought. Nicky adopted a Mona Lisa smile and I wondered if I was sporting a Mona Lisa scowl.

"You're a smart girl Sam. I always admired that about you. You never had to make anything up. Surely you can figure this out."

I looked Nicky up and down, mostly to buy myself some time. My mind began to wander – her style today was more Dragon's Den than Baghdad Barbie; a black blazer, a blouse cut to just above boob level (what a coincidence) and a pencil skirt that was so tight that it made her walk like she permanently needed a wee.

"I sort out...arrangements like yours all the time," Nicky said as she casually skewered her heel into the ground. "You almost had me fooled for a while, but I saw you off conspiring and knew you had hired Dean to pretend to be your boyfriend."

"I didn't hire him!" I blurted.

"Your payment scheme is really none of my business," Nicky said with a discreet wink. "Whatever it is, you've had a bargain. Dean will make a lot more on my books. Of course, I take a cut – we've just launched an app and I have to pay for that too, you know. But he won't be doing too badly at all." She seemed to consider the matter closed and began to walk away. "Oh," she remembered, "You will of course still get a very competitive rate if you ever decide to use the service. Look it up - it's called Bae for Pay."

It's easy to get caught up in a fantasy. I felt shame for how I had mercilessly mocked Nicky over the years for her inability to live in reality.

"Well, I'll leave you to it, then. I'm going to go and find a rock to go crawl under and die of embarrassment," I said, storming away from her.

I lurched up the stairs to our room, reeling but determined to pack as quickly as possible and get out of there.

Chapter 27

Dean was sitting on the edge of his bed packing his bag.

"I've just had a very interesting chat with Nicky," I said after I closed the door, my voice as soft as a silencer.

Dean held up his hands in resignation. When he saw my face in the mirror he began to pack his bag more quickly. I stared at him and he began to shift uncomfortably.

"It sounds like the start of your brilliant career."

Dean let a scrunched-up sock fall from his hand.

"Things happen."

"Things happen? That's a button falling off your jacket or losing your keys, not deciding to become a gigolo because you almost went an entire weekend without appearing disgusted by me. It's past 'things happen' – it's really more in 'shit went down' territory."

"I had a great time this weekend," he resumed his packing. "And that's why I made the choice."

I touched a hand to my head, I could feel my eyes rolling back and wanted to make sure they didn't get lodged in the depths of my cranium.

"I thought you were genuinely a bit torn last night?" I said.

"Oh, I was. That bit was real," he said, pensively wringing his piano tie. "The rest of it was fake."

He stuffed it unceremoniously into his bag. "Paxton is a bit...much for anyone who isn't a child soldier on a cocktail of cocaine and banned soft drinks."

"I thought you liked him?"

"That's how good I am," he smiled.

"At acting?"

"Well, yes," he threw the bag over his shoulder. "It's not the RSC but it's not stocking wine shelves either. I'm still playing dress up, I'm adored..."

"Ok, Pretty Woman."

Dean ignored the comment.

"Wait a minute," I said, rummaging in my pockets. "Perhaps I can find a fiver to pay you to laugh at that."

"It's now or never for me-"

"Oh sorry, you're Bon Jovi, I see now," I pouted.

"What did you want to happen? Us falling into each other's arms and running off to start a vineyard in the South of France? Tell me, because I never knew what you wanted," he said, folding his arms.

"I don't know," I said in a small voice. "It would have been nice to find out, though." I shrugged and sat on my bed, looking down at my feet. Here I was, berating him for trying to work out what he wanted, when I didn't have a clue either.

He shook his head and hoisted his bag onto his back. "You will work it out somehow," he gave me a half-smile. "I've got to go, Nicky's going to give me a ride back to the city."

I looked up from the floor just in time to see Dean leave, stepping out into the light of the corridor like it was the spotlight of centre stage.

Chapter 28

I was back in work the next day, and I was almost glad when Sandra the CEO compared some copy I had written to the 'memoirs of an illiterate farmhand'; her insults at least took my mind off the disaster that was the weekend.

In fact, pretending to be normal at work provided a welcome distraction for most of the week. I inquired after people's children just so they would talk for an hour about how little Lee was going to be the country's next great karate champion or how Pearl was really mastering her third language at age five. I found the general babble drowned out some of the worse bits of the weekend when my mind started replaying them. I even did one of those free online courses the company was always nagging us to do to give the illusion of professional development and I can now photoshop Sandra the CEO's head onto the body of a dragon with aplomb.

All this positivity lasted until about Friday lunchtime. Normally, I would start looking forward to a visit to Divine Drinks after work around then. I couldn't face going in and seeing the memories of more fun times there. By about 3.45pm, I was definitely in a funk, looking up ways to fake your own death on Google and getting annoyed at how much effort all of them seemed to take.

Then Patience, reliable as ever, asked: "What are you doing this weekend?"

"Oh, you know, just chilling really, the usual." I normally trotted out this line like a seasoned pro, but I knew it was lacking a little conviction.

"You don't sound very sure," she needled, smelling gossip in the air.

"You're right Patience, I have recently been burned by a wine merchant who posed as my significant other then abandoned me for a career as a gigolo. I shall probably head straight to the off licence, have a small cry by the cat litter, compose myself, buy the most disgusting bottle of Chardonnay they sell and lie on my bed in my pants looking up famous gigolos from history, concentrating particularly on those who have died from excruciating venereal diseases."

Patience had a fixed smile on her face, which I returned with a manic grin.

"Well dear, that is very honest of you. I'm no stranger to heartache myself. I've actually been having a wild affair with Duncan from Accounts, but his wife has found out and came round to my house the other day with a baseball bat threatening to kill me," Patience sighed, relieved. "Wow, it feels good to get that out there. Have a lovely weekend with the wine and Wikipedia, dear."

I watched Patience leave, not with her usual shuffle but a definite spring in her step. I was almost jealous of her, even if I found Duncan rather grotesque with his collection of vintage Barbies on his desk and permanent smell of rich tea biscuits. It had felt thrillingly subversive to actually tell a coworker what I was doing at the weekend, but it was short-lived for me and I could feel myself sinking as I walked home - via the off licence, of course.

I took a great deal of delight in scowling at Divine Drinks as I walked past. I presumed Dean no longer worked there but it still felt too soon to make my return. The urge to 'accidentally' knock over a row of their most expensive champagne and run out the shop was just too strong.

I slunk into the off licence about an hour later. At least the off licence will always be a constant in your life, I thought; a special grimy shade of yellow, the air scented with tobacco and additives, the cast of characters a desperate company of gamblers, drinkers and other wishful thinkers.

The man behind the counter was heavily invested in his phone but didn't look like your typical crusty corner shop employee. His stubble was more designer than desperado and his tweed jacket more Topman than 'I've just been kicked out of Ladbrokes for screaming about the whippets too much'. He was probably destined for things beyond doling out fags to dubious teenagers and elderly gentlemen. Nicky might snap him up too, my mind bitterly carried on.

My face was clearly betraying sour thoughts as I realised the attention had finally been wrenched from his phone. I buried my eyes in the juddering wine fridge as if it was a highbrow bookshop shelf. I settled on a Sauvignon Blanc that didn't look too poisonous and had a pony on the label.

I sighed heavily, it just wasn't as inventive as I'm Sorry Rosé or Sex, but it would have to do. The man at the counter glanced briefly at the bottle and mechanically punched the price into the till. I thought about how Dean and I would have hotly debated the topic of putting a pony on the bottle and mocked its no doubt vinegary vintage.

"£6.99," the man said, his eyes firmly locked on YouTube's '50 funniest car crashes'.

"Talking of car crashes, I've recently run over a group of children on a zebra crossing," I said cheerily. His eyes didn't shift. I put a £5 note on the counter and left unchallenged.

The automatic door didn't open for me and I thought he might have put the place on lockdown. However, the door then opened for a teenage mum and her three kids and I slipped out, unnoticed and wondering what it means when even the automatic doors don't acknowledge you.

Chapter 29

I was glad that the St Fillian's lot hadn't tried to get in touch after the reunion, apart from Paxton sending me his favourite classical art memes. No doubt Nicky had told them all something of the situation, and I really didn't want to deal with the gossip. I got away with this for three months or so, and then my phone rang. Harriet. Again. I couldn't avoid her forever, so I decided to bite the bullet and answer the phone.

At first, the conversation meandered around how unseasonably cold it was in their part of the country, Allan's new car and Harriet's decision to paint the living room an eggshell colour.

"And how are you?" Harriet asked in a sing-song voice.

"Oh good. Really busy," I replied as I absently gazed at a repeat of some reality show on a Saturday afternoon.

"Good, good." There was a pause that I was obviously meant to fill. "We have some news."

"Oh?"

"We are having a baby!"

"That's nice," I muttered. A perma-tanned blonde lady on the TV bitch-slapped a slightly less perma-tanned blonde lady. It was very engrossing.

"'That's nice?' Sam, it is the miracle of life and all I have wanted since I myself was a baby." The image was a little odd, but I would allow Harriet the dramatic licence.

“I’m sorry Harriet. That’s really great news for you,” I mustered.

“Sam - you sound distracted.”

“Sorry, I’m watching a really interesting documentary.”

“Sam, I am worried about you, even though I am pleased you are expanding your horizons with a documentary. Have you spoken to Dean since that weekend?”

“No, I don’t know what Nicky has told you, but we are just going in different directions. I am concentrating on improving myself. You know, watching documentaries and the like.” The perma-tanned blonde ladies were now grabbing each other by the hair.

Harriet mumbled, disapprovingly, of course. “Sam, I have to go. Mothercare has a sale on and I need to get one of those new prams so I can stick it to the other mums at nursery one day. I am so excited!”

Harriet hung up and I went back to watching the cat fight.

Chapter 30

Some time later, mostly thanks to the shameful glares I was getting from Lily the cat (she was still not over the Christmas card incident, it would seem), I extricated myself from the sofa and groaned as my back made various crunching and clicking noises. A massage was probably in order, and June was due back from an impromptu expedition to Bhutan with Professor P in a few days. However, another woman who worked part-time in June's shop was running things while she was away, so I could still book an appointment for June's return. Actually speaking to someone on the phone suddenly seemed like a sensory overload and I felt very fragile and millennial; it was almost too much social contact to provide the online booking form with my phone number. What if they phone me and I actually have to talk to someone? Would they eventually give up and text me instead? I could feel another knot develop in my shoulder as I brooded.

I was surprised when it was June who replied with an email; internet was really spotty in the remote area where the Prof was doing fieldwork. 'Hey comrade! Finally found decent wifi - one day before we come back! That's you booked in, can't wait to catch up on everything! See you on Friday. PS Workers of the world unite xoxo'

That Friday, Patience asked me once again what I was doing at the weekend.
"Getting a massage from a Thai lady."

She raised her eyebrows. "Gigolos and exotic massages. You work next to someone for four years and it turns out you don't know them at all," she muttered as she left.

Chapter 31

A waft of essential oils hit me as I opened the shop door. Surrounded by fragrant candles and Buddha statues, June studied A Guide to Oriental Marxism in Modern Art intensely.

She only looked up when she finished her page, then she flew across the room and gave me a huge hug. "Sam! It's you! I'm sorry, I was just so engrossed in my book." A misty look entered her eyes. "Professor P gave it to me."

"That's very romantic, in an academic kind of way."

"Isn't it?" she trilled, now hugging the book to her chest. She gazed down at it for a few moments. "Your massage!" She finally remembered.

I undressed to the tune of Thai elevator muzak, which June was humming along to.

"This one is on the house, as a small thank you for introducing me to Professor P," she said in the '70s hippy tone massage therapists adopt as soon as they begin their work.

"So just chill and relax."

"I've never known how to do that."

"Just empty your mind of all thoughts."

"But then it will just be the little voice that tells me that I am unworthy of love or success and should throw myself in the nearest river immediately."

June kneaded my shoulders thoughtfully. "Perhaps I should turn up the music to drown that out too?"

"That would be nice."

The tinkling music surged louder for a moment, the Asian string instruments morphing into an imitation of Highway to Hell. The muscles in my back knotted in defence.

"Made you jump," giggled June. "It's amazing what you can find with a bit of googling - including AC/DC for Relaxation."

"Well, this isn't the relaxing experience promised by the stock image of the white lady wearing nothing but a towel and a smile on your flyer, June."

"I thought it would make you laugh," she placed a reassuring hand on my back. "I just want to make you smile, even if your face is smooshed into a pillow just now."

I was glad the pillow was there to absorb the tear or two that had been brewing in my eyes. I would just have to tell June that I had drooled a little, I resolved. The rest of the massage passed in silence, well, apart from the mood music.

When I emerged from the massage room, June was already once again engrossed in her book. She barely looked up as I entered the reception. However, the grumble of a car engine outside made her prick up her ears. Professor P's cream convertible drove straight out of the '80s and into view.

He vaulted over the top and leaned against the hood, fishing a cigarette out of his jacket pocket. Who said men couldn't multi-task?

June waved at him coyly.

"Tell him I'll be five minutes. I need to close up," she said to me, ostensibly, but her eyes were fixed on him. Out in the street, Professor P lowered his sunglasses and peered at me through a plume of smoke.

"She'll be five minutes," I said, making for a brisk exit.

"Well, you can surely keep me company for five minutes, then," he shrugged. I waited silently, like a naughty child staring at the clock in detention. "We once had an entire debate about whether Man Ray or Hieronymous Bosch would win in a fight. I don't believe you're the sort to run out of things to say."

I mimed a smile.

"June told me what happened between you and Dean."

I rolled my eyes in exasperation, almost tempted to break my vow of silence.

"Now, I will say that I cannot see why you have got yourself in such a funk. You essentially had a free concubine to make yourself look good in front of a bunch of ossified middle-class farts. That's a service I would and have paid good money for."

"Yes, Roxette was an interesting addition to the 2013 department barbeque," I conceded.

Professor P smiled nostalgically. "My favourite part was when one of her breasts almost took out the Vice Principal's eye."

"You should do something to get over it. Not that!" he said with a needling wiggle of his eyebrows.

"I don't know what you mean," I said. I pulled my phone out of my jacket pocket and pretended to send a text; I needed something to distract from the shade of gazpacho my cheeks were going. I did know what Professor P was talking about, but I had tried to forget it, like I had everything else connected to Ray.

It was a couple of weeks after the twin events of graduation and Ray dumping me for a career as an adventuring sex memoirist when it happened. Harriet and I had gone out on the town and I drank so much tequila that a rebound shag with Professor P seemed like a good idea. St Fillan's being smaller than a large shopping mall, I soon found him on our pub crawl. My tequila-fuelled overtures were rejected, in part due to their incoherency and a crude diagram I vaguely remember drawing on a beer mat. He also said I was in a state and it would be 'wrong', this coming from a man who once painted an antelope-spider hybrid.

The next morning I woke up with a horrendous hangover and sense of shame; not only had I tried it on with the Letchy Lecturer in Chief, but he had rejected me. The same man who would probably be sexually attracted to a water buffalo if you put it in some yoga pants and a St Fillan's hoodie. It was all so embarrassing that I couldn't even tell June about it, and even at the time, Harriet had been given a very PG version of events.

She still felt sorry for me though - when we went to visit Paxton in Maine, she insisted on setting me up with the lifeguard on Paxton's private beach, which ended up being a much less messy rebound than it would have been with the professor, but I still felt incredibly awkward about the tequila episode.

"My lips are sealed. I haven't said anything to June," he whispered. "But you should do something to get it out of your system. Do you still write?"

"Just reports that make me want to eat my own hands," I said, stuffing my phone back into my pocket.

Professor P locked his cigarette in a tight smile. "Try and find something that makes you happy," he said and I gave him a sceptical glance. "You might even surprise everyone and actually enjoy yourself!" I threw him a gurn straight out of the grumpy teenager handbook.

June tumbled out the shop, shortly followed by her dog. "I'm coming! I'm coming! Sorry, I picked up my book again and just had to finish the chapter."

"Aren't you glad I recommended it?" The professor wrapped an arm around her, the other supporting them against the hood.

"You'll have to make me a reading list at this rate," laughed June. Leni barked approvingly. It was quite sickening.

"I'll see what I can do. Shall we?" Professor P stubbed out his fag.

"Yes!" June bounded round to the passenger seat with Leni following in hot pursuit.

"Do something. Be happy," Professor P said to me with a departing peck on the cheek. His words and the tobacco smell lingered for a long time.

Chapter 32

A few days later, Paxton sent me another meme. I thought about just replying with a crying-laughing emoji, like I had done the last six or seven times I discovered as I scrolled through our chat history. Seeing all his messages made me realise it was months since we had spoken properly, so instead I replied with: "Miss you and your craziness. You free for a chat?"

A few seconds later my phone was ringing. I answered and Paxton's pixelated face materialised on my screen. A juddering voice to match struggled out of my phone.

"Sam!" I presume he said.

"Paxton, your connection is crap," I annunciated.

The screen smudged to a Monet painting for a few seconds.

"That better?" asked Paxton, suddenly appearing in acute detail.

"I can see you, which doesn't make it better, to be honest."

I could see the sun glinting in the back of the image and a sandy beach snaking its way into the foreground. My British sofa somehow felt chillier and I hugged my duvet closer.

"You're so cute and bitter," said Paxton.

"I'm not Humphrey Bogart reincarnated as a puppy," I grumbled.

He sipped a glass of white wine, dripping with condensation.

"What are you drinking?" I asked.

"I don't know but it's delicious, which, coincidentally, also the name of this fine lady." A woman of indeterminate race – like the final superhuman when ethnicity has become moot - appeared behind him. Exotic flowers were so entwined in her hair that they looked like they were growing out of her head.

"You've certainly gone up in the world since Harriet and Allan."

"Well, they had their charms. Well, Harriet had her charms. When I squinted and pretended she was a lusty tavern wench from the 1800s."

"I've always admired your creativity."

"I have a lot to hand to Harriet and Allan, actually. Our ménage à trois made me realise something."

A moment of profound silence followed. I wondered what it could be - he was wasting his life as a louche dilettante? It was time for him to become a one-woman man and move to the suburbs and raise the next generation of little weirdos?

"I was made for threesomes."

Delicious draped a hand, which looked like a female version of God's in a Michelangelo fresco, over Paxton's shoulder. At least, that's what I thought it was, until the face of another equally divine woman popped onto the screen.

"You know me, Sam, I am a very giving person, I'm a great admirer of beauty, and, as luck would have it, I have found kindred spirits in the celestial shapes of Delicious and Monique. It's time for me to say, 'take that, society'! You know what I'm talking about. Do you remember that time you reviewed the Fine Wine and Cheese Society's Salute to France in the character of a French revolutionary?"

"I had smelly cheese shoved through my letter box for a week after that. I'm not sure if it was a compliment or not."

"Well, you did liken the cheese to the rotting, bloated corpses of the bourgeoisie, so..."

Paxton trailed off. Monique and Delicious were obviously growing bored and were playfully pinging each other's bikini straps.

"You should get back to your comrades. You can't free love all by yourself."

"You're so smart. Things are going to work out for you Sam, I just know it. Monique, don't open that coconut with your thighs yet - wait for me!"

The screen turned black.

Chapter 33

The next day was staring at the blank page in front of me. No change there - it was a pretty normal Friday afternoon in the office. I took stock of the various reasons my colleagues had given for leaving early - a dentist appointment (the third this week), 'brainstorming' (in the pub) and a sick child (despite being childless) and I considered starting the report on the Analytics of KPIs and Business Needs, but then I remembered no one would probably read it anyway. In fact, they would probably be far too busy adapting to life without teeth, or their very sudden parenthood, or setting up their satellite office in the local Wetherspoons.

Then I thought about what everyone else would be doing right now. Harriet was probably dragging Allan around Mothercare, June was more than likely on an idyllic Thai island exchanging furtive glances and sociological theories with Professor P, and Nicky and Dean I could see rolling around in the profits of ill-gotten gains on a heart-shaped bed, with a queue of lonely women waiting at the door.

Where was I? I was still in the office on a Friday afternoon. Once Harriet, Paxton and I had compiled a book of reasons to go to the pub instead of revise but now I couldn't even summon enough creativity to bugger off before 5pm.

Someone plodded down the corridor. Startled, I began to type randomly in case they popped their head in on their way to their own 'dentist appointment'. It was a cleaner, but she was obviously determined to finish as soon as possible, grimly hoovering a stubborn spot on the floor before moving off with purpose.

Looking at the jumble of letters on the screen, I realised I could do something to almost, sort of, right this mess. I pressed delete and watched the letters smoothly disappear.

Now I only had to fill the document once more - with my own story. Ok, so it might never be as good as my Fine Wine and Cheese review, but it would still be an accomplishment, right?

So every Friday afternoon I would sit typing feverishly at my desk, to the admiring and slightly fearful glances of coworkers off to various appointments that somehow always fell at 2.30pm on a Friday. If everyone else was taking care of themselves, and they certainly were if they apparently had three dental appointments a week, then so could I.

Sometimes I would look up from the keyboard to see that the time had well and truly crept past 5 o'clock and I would pack up my things, satisfied after a day's hard work. Finally, this was some personal development I could get on board with. I felt like I had much more purpose doing this than photoshopping Sandra the CEO's head onto dragons. I would read paragraphs back to myself and feel the pages come to life, instead of giving them the last rites before putting another dull corporate press release into the world. Maybe I was good at writing, no matter what Sandra insisted on saying at any given opportunity, I would think as I locked up the office for the night.

Afterwards I would stop in at the off licence to pick up a bottle of wine as a reward. Not once in those months did the same guy behind the till ever look up to see me, but, I cautioned myself, that was probably a good thing given what had happened the last time. Although I knew that I couldn't truly be angry or upset with Dean and Nicky – they had provided me with a wealth of material, after all. Sometimes I would wonder where they were, but as time went on, I was looking to the story I wanted to tell more and more, marching them through the plot like my pawns instead of the other way round.

It wasn't always easy, though. There were nights I would return home from work, exhausted – clearly on days when there were no dentist appointments to be had and the imaginary children were in robust health. There my screen would stare at me as blankly as I would at it and the only inspiration I found was in cutting myself down to size. Who was I to think I could write a book? So what if I had written a pithy article or two that had moved some to laughter and others to cheese-based hate crimes? That didn't make me Jane Austen or Dorothy Parker, it made me like the countless others who had dashed something off for their student newspaper and promptly faded into an office job upon graduation.

Usually after the second glass of wine, I began to feel a bit more optimistic. If E.L. James could be a published author, then why not me? I wouldn't even put any bad S&M in my sex scenes, I was already ahead of her. Then there was that guy from university who had self-published a fantasy series on Amazon - currently sitting at 35 downloads- mostly by myself and Paxton (we do dramatic readings to each other of - you guessed it - the badly written sex scenes). If he could do it, then why not me? I would be happy with 35 downloads and being mercilessly mocked by my peers, anything to taste the sweet nectar of being semi-relevant.

So I would carry on typing, punching the keys as doggedly as the cleaner dragged the hoover over the same spots of the otherwise deserted office, week in, week out.

Chapter 34

When I had written up enough that I was sure that Paxton could get a good laugh at it in between vigorous love sessions with Delicious and Monique, I sent him a copy.

Then the dread set in. It felt like the worst hangover fear ever – like I had thought it would be a good idea to send him nudes after one too many and was now waiting on his reply, knowing that a bottle of I'm Sorry Rosé could not cleanse the sins of this one.

Each day that went by without a reply, I read into my empty inbox in lieu of any reading material from Paxton. In my more optimistic moments, I desperately reasoned that perhaps he was on yet another exotic vacation with his concubines. Then I would slip down an anxiety well and decided that Paxton was offended by his portrayal and making a Sam voodoo doll to stab thoroughly.

So I went back to whiling away Friday afternoons trying to beat my personal best for a lap of the office in my wheelie chair. Sometimes my phone would light up with an email, but it was always a local takeaway sensing my weakness for a 15% off voucher, or the wine shop with an automated 'We miss you!' email. I saw a notification and my eyes filled in the blanks - a '15% off pizza and sides' headlines was already in my mind, but it was not the Pizza Shack luring me in with its Siren's Call. 'Hillary Paxton' (yes, Hillary, there is a reason he goes by his surname), Re: writing'. I swiped the notification away like it was a bat that had just flown into my face. I debated not opening it at all. Did I really need to be confronted with my own inferiority? I could just burn my laptop when I got home to rid myself once and for all of any literary ambitions and this obvious flop that was stinking out my Documents folder.

After a bit of pacing (OK, nervous rolling in the chair), I decided to expose myself to the contents of the email. If all my hopes were to be dashed, they might as well be extinguished completely with some hurtful phrases I could summon up at will whenever I felt a burst of self-confidence coming on.

I took a long, condemned breath and opened my email application. The email preview began 'Wow...' 'Wow' what, I wondered? 'Wow...you should be sectioned? Or 'Wow...you are a broken shell of a woman, please seek professional help immediately'? Or worse, 'Wow...' alone. With one last anxious gulp, I pressed 'open'.

> Wow, Sam. I loved it. I felt like I was there, maybe because I was? This 'Paxton' fella seems like a total stud. I'm serious though, it's good, and I'm not just saying that like the time Nicky let me read her 'memoirs' from her time as a CIA agent. In all fairness to her though, it was probably the greatest work of fiction I have ever read. Anyway, enough about that witch, who you have very vividly brought to life, by the way.
>
> I am back in the UK next week to meet up with my Uncle Ed. I say he is my uncle, but what do you call a man who was once married to your ex-stepmother? That whole story is probably a book in itself. Anyway, I digress - long and short of it is that Uncle Ed has something to do with publishing that I don't really understand and he is very discerning - he has repeatedly refused to publish my growing collection of erotic limericks and love ballads dedicated exclusively to the goddess that is Cher. As you will know from the many dramatic readings that I have given you over the years, it really is ground-breaking stuff. However, Ed is not a fan and says it is a product of a 'disturbed mind' and I should 'seek help immediately before it is too late'. Some people are just prudes. He is a prude who knows what's good though - I took the liberty of sending him a couple of chapters and in his words, he 'laughed, cried and paused for thought - and not in the way your awful worrying poetry does, Paxton.' As I said, prude.
>
> He has invited me for drinks at the Tollcross Book Club on Thursday and wants you to come too - says he wants to see the woman behind the madness and introduce you to some people. What do you say?
>
> Yours, spiritually, physically and emotionally (for one night only if you ever want me), P

I felt like I had been in a car crash after reading Paxton's missive. A semi-pleasant car crash - one you survive with only one or two life-altering injuries, but a car crash nonetheless. I left it in my inbox for a while, waiting for the battered and bruised feeling to subside. I remember walking around the supermarket a bit blankly, finding myself at the crappy book rack, full of bargain basement thrillers and unarousing bonk busters. Maybe my own name would stare down upon unsuspecting shoppers one day. I wasn't sure why - my story had absolutely no commercial appeal and only speaks to a selection of millennials who can't afford to buy it anyway. Another thing I wasn't sure about was how I felt about sharing my work more widely, even with my friends. Did I want to open myself up to the possibility of even more rejection and scrutiny than I got working for Sandra? Just like nobody likes the sound of their own voice, they dislike themselves even more in print - and hate the writer most of all for their portrait.

Later I returned to my inbox, cautiously typing and untyping until I arrived at this:

> Hi Paxton,
>
> I am so glad you liked my writing. 'Glad' is maybe the wrong word - relieved is probably better. If you hadn't, I would have probably had to commit seppuku and it doesn't rhyme with much, so it would be hard for you to immortalise me in a limerick.
>
> I [the next bit I variously deleted and rewrote several times with a few Facebook breaks] would love to meet up with you and your 'Uncle' on Thursday. See you at the Tollcross Book Club [I tried to write this bit as calmly as possible - as if the Tollcross Book Club was not the same place as where Hemingway once got in a heated argument with Colette about who could seduce the most women in the one evening].
>
> I will try and clear my very busy schedule as an office drone if you kindly let me know the time of our rendezvous.

Over the next few days I practiced my best odious literary laugh and tried to cobble something together from my wardrobe that said 'refined writer' rather than 'these leggings have holes in them and that's why I am leaning against this wall'. I had never been in the Tollcross Book Club and had only had fleeting glimpses in its windows on my commute. At first, these moments weren't much use - all I ever saw was an impenetrable barricade of Chesterfield furniture and cigar smoke. Then it began to dawn on me that that was all

I needed to know; there wasn't a place for me there, not even if I groped around in the cigar fog for a spare seat. There was no way 'Uncle Ed' would make it all the way out to my flat - he sounded far more gentry than gentrification. Perhaps we could meet halfway.

I fired off a revised reply:

> Paxton - slight change of plan. I won't be able to make it to Tollcross, due to a mixture of not wanting to and an entrenched British classist inferiority complex. Instead, I'll be at the wine shop where it all began and hope you will be too. Don't reply - I want to have one last good anxiety attack before the fateful day.

Chapter 35

That Thursday night I set off feeling not dread at my return, but feeling thankful. I was thankful I had someone like Paxton who was always fearless when I was fearful, and for June and Professor P for showing me it was never too late to live your dream. Harriet and Allan had shown me you can get what you want - it's just that sometimes that it happens in a roundabout way.

I was smiling to myself when I felt someone smiling back at me. I realised who it was and mine began to shrink. Theirs did too, but I fixed mine back on.

"Dean!" I exclaimed.

"Sam," a different, thinner smile appeared - I thought he was meant to be a good actor! His companion looked equally worried and reminded me of someone - me a few months ago; worrying the jig is up and the world knows you have a man for hire. There was another reason she looked familiar though - I had worked beside her for four years, even if she still claimed to think my name was Simon.

"Sandra...the CEO!" I said, unable to contain a morbidly delighted grin. It all made sense now - her steady stream of companions had clearly been provided by Bae for Pay. I kicked myself for not immediately recognising her, depriving myself of a few more seconds to bask in her mortification. I was being hard on myself though, it's always strange when you see coworkers outside the office, especially with an on-duty gigolo.

"You know each other?" she said, suppressing a gag. Clearly she paid for her Friday night companions to come from better stock.

Oh, it was another time, another place, as they say," I said, a little sadly, even though it was giving me some perverse pleasure to watch Dean squirm.

"It's a nice night, isn't it?" Dean blurted.

I imagined this was the sort of non-sequitur that would come out if an Alexa had a stroke.

"Better than I ever expected it to be. I hope you're both well."

A film of perspiration was forming on Sandra the CEO's perfectly waxed upper lip as she realised just how much I knew.

"I'm good, thanks for asking," I carried on brightly. Thinking of Professor P, I opted for a different phrase, "Actually, I'm happy. Yes, I'm happy. For so many reasons tonight," I said, trying and failing to suppress a grin.

"And how do you two know each other?" asked Dean, clearly drawing straight from a handbook of polite conversation issued by Nicky.

"Sandra is the CEO of the company I work for!"

Dean did the mental maths and joined his beau in the Sweaty Upper Lip Club.

"Yes. What a small world," I said, dry as a Sauvignon Blanc.

"What are your plans tonight, then?" asked Sandra the CEO begrudgingly, staring down at her Nazi boots. "Learning to read and write, finally?" she said, finding her stride and a smirk.

"I'm off to the wine shop," I began to walk away, "It's funny, some people never change, do they?"

And with that, I turned away and never looked back.

ACKNOWLEDGEMENTS

They say writing is a solitary pursuit, but Bae for Pay wouldn't be in your hands if it wasn't thanks to the help and support of a lot of people.

My family:

My Gran, Irene Barrett, deserves thanks for always encouraging me to tell stories, from the elaborate soap operas we used to act out with my Barbies through to today. My parents, Eva Barrett and Gordon Steel, have been incredibly supportive and enthusiastic about me writing and publishing this, which cements the status they have always had as the 'cool parents'.

Thank you to my partner Rob and our furry children Iris and Titus for always being there for me, whether I'm smashing the latest milestone or having a wee existential cry about everything. They are always on hand with calming cuddles and/or a glass of wine, the latter often supplied by the kindly wine merchants of Leith.

My friends:

The Clash of the Titus and The Sassy Ladies groups have championed me throughout the process. Particular thanks must go to Charlotte Reid and Calum Craig for their advice and promotional help, stepping up as an event organiser (Charlotte) and model/proofreader (Calum).

Felix Kaplan also acted as both a wise and hilarious proofreader for the novel. I might write another just to get his comments. We met at St Andrews a decade ago and thanks are due to the University for bringing so many brilliant people into my life, including the luscious Lucy Gallard, who created original artwork based on the book.

Thank you to Cara Becker for creating a wonderful website and always being willing to meet me somewhere in Europe.

Many colleagues from my day job gave encouragement and advice when I shared my work (especially Sarah Ford-Hutchinson), inspiring me to take it to the next level, even in my many colourful moments of self-doubt.

The professionals:

Though I would like to think these people are also firmly in the 'friend' category, their professional expertise has been invaluable.

Sibyl Adam acted as an incredible editor, pushing me to create the best novel possible and kicking me firmly out of my comfort zone (in the nicest possible way).

A big thank you to Paul Storie at Storie&Storie for working his design magic on this and for always being up for bouncing ideas about, even during a pandemic.

Becca Coffey of Blush has helped me manage full-time work and writing over the last year, giving me great strategies for tackling everything from self-care to self-publishing. Thanks for being my 'professional friend'!

Teuchters Landing deserves a mention for not only being a great bar but a great venue for taking headshots with Andrew Perry.

In fact, Andrew's photography has really captured the essence of Bae for Pay (now you've finished the book, flick back to the front cover to see what I mean).